Long Blows the North Wind

Brian McCulloch's only friend and partner is gunned down by Jason Grier and his prowling gang after they set upon the pair, hoping to steal a cartload of valuable furs.

To avenge his friend and to prove himself a man, Brian needs to track down Grier . . . but the trail is long and cold, and the storms he must pass through are more violent than he could have ever expected.

2

Long Blows the North Wind

Owen G. Irons

A Black Horse Western

ROBERT HALE · LONDON

ISBN 978-0-7090-8947-6

Robert Hale Limited
Clerkenwell House
Clerkenwell Green
London EC1R 0HT

www.halebooks.com

Typeset by
Derek Doyle & Associates, Shaw Heath
Printed and bound in Great Britain by
CPI Antony Rowe, Chippenham and Eastbourne

ONE

We knew early that it was going to be a hard winter. Thousands of geese were winging their way southward in long, graceful 'V's, the leafy trees had begun dropping their foliage in a whirlwind of color, and the pelts we were taking were thick and heavy.

Which was all a profitable sign for Sad Sam and me; that is, the prime fox and beaver we were trapping up along the Milk River would fetch a fine price in the East. Only thing was, neither of us was in a mood to linger through another long Montana winter.

The year before, we had had snowdrifts ten feet high outside the only window of our log shanty and we had not only nearly frozen but driven each other half crazy, retelling old stories and old longings hunched over a low-glowing fire in the stone hearth.

Not that Sad Sam and I weren't the best of friends, but spend four winter months locked in a twelve-by-twelve cabin with your dearest of friends and you will understand what I mean.

We were not of a mind to repeat the experience.

'Brian,' Sad Sam said as he sat on the bench before our hut, looking up at the cold Montana skies on this late September day, 'we have done well enough for ourselves. Besides, the foxes are soon going to take to their dens, the beaver to their lodges. I've had about enough of the north country for a time, and – excuse me – enough of your company.'

I couldn't argue with the old man; he was right. We had been trapping along the river for eighteen months, sometimes half-frozen, always half-hungry. It was time we gave it up.

'There's flatboats going downriver along the Missouri now, all the way to Saint Jo,' Sad Sam was saying kind of dolefully as he tried to strike fire to his curved-stem pipe. 'Why don't we take what furs we have and "beat feet"?'

By which he meant arrange our fortunes so that we were somewhere in the southern climes before the first blizzard of winter hit.

I agreed.

Sad Sam was as close to me as a father, but the prospect of spending another long winter locked up together inside a smoky, airless cabin was beyond consideration. We agreed to depart from the Montana land on that September day in the year 1876.

I have to take a moment to explain about Sam and myself.

Sad Sam McCulloch had taken me under his wing when, as a youngster, our wagon train had been hit by Sioux Indians, leaving very few on either side alive. My parents were among the dead, I discovered, when I crawled out of the poor shelter where I had hidden at the first sound of a war whoop.

I don't suppose many of you would be interested in the details – it was so long ago, and I was too young to remember it all. The killing, that is. But Sam was there, an army scout in his greasy buckskins, and he took me from beneath a burning wagon and nurtured me. As I say, that is a different, long story; I just wanted to explain how Sad Sam and I came to be where we were and why I was so close to him.

There we were, on this fine Montana morning, the sky high and impossibly long and there were magpies in the meadow, and a clump of crows in the pines, and far away a small herd of elk, and I wondered if I could bear to leave this country of enormous beauty and heartbreak, but I knew it was the thing to do.

We piled the pelts onto the two-wheeled cart we had. Then we backed old 'Ben' our black mule into the traces, I threw a saddle on my feisty four-year-old sorrel gelding, Santana, and we started for the Missouri River, sorry to be leaving, but relieved at the same time, for the snows were not far behind us.

If I have not already said this – I'm kind of new to this writing game – my name is Brian McCulloch. I'm twenty years old, at a rough guess, my parents being dead and unable to vouch for that. I have sort of coppery-brown hair and stand a notch under six feet tall.

That's about all there is to know about me, I guess, except what I have mentioned above. I am no stronger built than usual. That is, a man who spends his bringing-up years chopping timber and tramping the high north country is naturally going to be broader than some Philadelphia clerk. But that is only a matter of experience and of necessity. There are some bear-like men up here in Montana, but I am not a man with a build like an ox and the temper of a catamount.

To get back to what I was telling you, we were proceeding toward the Upper Missouri hoping to catch ferry transport south. Our cart was piled high with prime furs and we hoped to reach St Joseph or St Louis before the ice floes clogged the big river. We had some concern about the Indians, but the Cheyenne had been quiet and from what we had heard at the trading posts, the Nez Perce had begun to emigrate to Canada.

Besides, Sad Sam knew many of the local tribes. He had always treated them with respect, and in turn they had treated us well.

What we didn't expect was a band of white raiders wanting our wealth in furs.

The pine forest we were passing though was tall and cool and blue. There were patches of thin snow reflecting the afternoon light which sprayed like sifting gold through the trees. There was no sound but the steady creaking of the cart's wheels and the twisting of the wind through the lodgepole pines. Sam, who could hear a bird whisper at a hundred yards, did not hear them coming. I, whose thoughts were on a long-ago vision of a girl I never knew, did not see them on the pine-clad ridge

There were six of them,. And they knew what they wanted. Furs were going at a prime rate in those times;

beaver, especially. Men from New York to London were crazy to have beaver hats. I don't know why exactly; I just knew that trapping them was a way to keep bread in our mouths.

When the bandits came down on us from out of the darkness of the pines, they shot Sam through the lungs.

They were a fur-clad bunch of bearded men with evil intentions. Could I have resisted more? I don't know. Their leader rode his big bay horse up to me before I could even draw my Colt or unsheathe my Henry 'Yellow Boy' rifle, and he clubbed me down. As I hit the pine-needle-strewn ground I wondered if I could fight back, but I didn't see how with half a dozen mounted armed men around me.

Still I wondered if I was a coward. I could see Sad Sam as he lay dying, his mouth filled with blood.

'Do you wish to die or to live?' a man asked me. A huge, dark-bearded bull-shouldered man with glittering black eyes.

'Live . . .' I managed to say and cursed myself for it. Sam no longer twitched or spoke, or breathed. But his eyes seemed to meet mine for one final moment and I was so ashamed that I wished I had chosen the alternative and said, 'I wish to die.'

That, my friends, is what began my odyssey. Shame and doubts about my own manhood.

I am not proud of the surge of revenge that slowly grew within me. It is an unjustifiable emotion.

But murder is more inexcusable. To those of you who have never lived in a world where a man is his own administrator of justice because there is no other law, where there is no authority to appeal to, what follows might seem cruel or brutal, but in those times, in Montana territory I was the only law and my only friend had been murdered by these thieves simply for profit.

I could not let that pass unanswered.

I knew the man commanding them, Jason Grier. He had come by once in the heart of winter and been welcomed to our table. Sam had no liking for the man, but in those old days, no one was turned away from the door hungry.

As I have said, I carried a Colt revolver on my hip, but I had never fired it in anger. Once I had shot it into the air to frighten away a prowling and too-familiar grizzly bear, but it was carried more as a matter of custom than as a defense. Maybe that is why I did not draw my gun when Jason Grier hovered over me, looking through me with those mean coyote eyes. I don't know. I always hoped it was because I was not a coward, but I felt as if I was in the days that followed.

I watched the cart with our furs be drawn away, I watched Jason's last disparaging over-the-shoulder glance at me; watched Santana being led away. Then on elbows and knees I dragged myself to where Sad Sam lay dying.

He lifted a bloody hand as if he wished to clasp my own, but he hadn't the strength and his fingers fell away in a slow, futile gesture. I sat beside him; I closed his eyelids. The forest was thick and deeply shadowed, the blue of the spruce so deep a blue that they seemed black.

I sat there. My arms hung loosely and the chirping of

the forest birds seemed to pause and await resolution. I found none within me. I sat with the cold blue steel of my unfired revolver, itself accusing, on my lap.

I had done nothing to protect my only friend.

Now, it does not matter that nothing could really have prevented his death, but thoughts such as those linger in a man's mind. Shamefaced, I began to carve a shallow grave out of the dark soil, praying that the beasts would not find Sad Sam.

It was then, as I returned Sad Sam McCulloch to the earth and a raucous crow sounding high in the pines reminded me that I was kneeling alone in silent invocation, that I knew what must be done. I am not a vengeful man, but they had begun the war. With a weary sadness I rose from the earth as the first light snow began to fall. I knew what I had to do.

I would track the men responsible for this, and if I had to, I would kill them. It was not honor, nor hot pride, nor a vengeance-lust swelling within me. It was a sense that only I, across those thousand miles of wild country, could bring any sort of justice to these killers.

I rose unsteadily and sorrowfully from the gravesite and lifted my eyes to the cold skies of Montana. I feared that I was about to become a killer myself, like it or not, a role I was not suited to either by skill or temperament.

Sad Sam was the only parent I had ever known. Together we hunted, fished, at times hid out from hostile Indians, built our ramshackle cabin along the Milk River, worked our small truck garden, trapped, ate and sometimes wrangled with each other as all close people do. I did not remember my father. I barely remember my mother. Sad Sam was all the family I had ever known. Old, grizzled, whiskey- and tobacco-smelling coot . . . well, I could tell you a lot more about the way Sam hand-raised me and tried to teach me right, but it would take more than a book. He became my father.

And my friend.

I dragged myself up from my knees before Sam's cold grave, maybe feeling sorrier for myself than I did for Sam – I don't know.

Our year's work was gone, our furs, but that didn't seem important. I was afoot in the middle of Montana Territory at the onset of winter – and that did matter. I stood straight, hands on hips, took a deep breath, looked around me at the deep forest and started walking, following the ruts the cart had left in the dark earth.

I thought I knew where Grier and his gang were headed. It had to be far-off St Joseph or even St Louis, because there was no place in the north country to sell such a quantity of furs. I considered tracking them as they proceeded southward, but afoot it was obviously hopeless. They would easily outdistance me. My second notion was to find the Missouri as we had planned all along and see if I couldn't out-race them to the civilized lands by traveling downriver. *How* I was to do it was a different question. Nevertheless, I turned my boots eastward and slogged my way forward through the day and into the bitter cold of the Montana evening.

I rose in the frosty morning as stiff as if I had slept in sin, stretched my bunched muscles and went on as the red sun hoisted itself above the eastern horizon. Rime crunched beneath my boots, steam issued from my lips as I tramped along my uncertain route. By noon I had reached a tributary of the Upper Missouri locally called the Yellow, though it was really an arm of the Milk River. I was weary, hungry and disheartened. My scheme seemed mad and futile.

I rested in the shade of the river oaks, watching idly as a high-flying crow circled above me. I was lost. Not because I was alone in the vastness of the plains – for that was where I had been nurtured – but because I had no real plan for survival. That is, I had always had Sad Sam, our successful if unpredictable trapping business, some sort of home and stability. Now I had nothing, nothing at all.

Dwelling on that was going to accomplish nothing. I rose from the ground and walked on through the blackthorn and willow brush, aware of the silver glint of the sun on the river, the whisper of the wind in the barren wide-spreading, oaks, the occasional splash of a rising fish.

I came upon the canoe half an hour on.

Birch-bark, Indian-made, it was tied to a riverside sycamore by means of a rawhide string. I glanced around warily, my hand on my holstered Colt. I crouched slightly and listened intently, but there seemed to be no one around. Unsheathing my bowie knife I cut the canoe's tether. Feeling like a thief I dragged the canoe to the water's edge. My conscience caught up with me as I shipped the canoe, and I returned to the cove where I had found it tethered. With an overhand thrust, I drove the blade of my bowie knife into the sycamore tree, and left it shimmering there in the early sunlight. Steel knives were still uncommon among the Indians, especially one of that quality. I hoped that whoever's canoe I had taken would accept it as a fair trade.

I shoved the canoe into the Yellow, took up the paddle and began making my slow way toward the wide Missouri.

TWO

The Milk River flows south and east until it meets the Upper Missouri a little north of Fort Peck. It runs gentle and wide most times, and now, as I drifted along its silver face, it was pleasant and peaceful. The river found its way through tall granite outcroppings split by freezing winters and spring thaws. Tall pines crowded the shore like interested spectators. There were only a few wisps of cloud high in the lonesome sky. The only sounds were the occasional splash of mallard ducks landing or departing, and the quiet dipping of my oar as I steered my way southward. There were deer along the shoreline, hundreds of them, and occasionally a moose. I spotted one grizzly bear carrying a silvery fish in its mouth. It glanced at me dismissively and shambled on its way.

After a few miles, the canoe began to leak.

A small trickle of water from a seam near the bow drew my attention. Frowning, I tried to plug the chink in the birch-bark with my neckerchief. Fingering the seam, I could feel that the pine resin used to seal the birch was old and brittle. Cursing my luck I steered

15

nearer to the shore in case the leak grew worse.

Almost immediately that did begin to happen, and worse turned to worst as the sections of birch bark began to separate themselves. I now paddled with all my strength, having no wish to go down in the frigid river. I barely made it to the gravel beach before the canoe virtually came apart at the seams. I stepped out onto the shore and sat on the ground, watching the canoe flood and sag into the water to die. There was a reason, then, that the canoe had been abandoned.

The Indian had gotten the better of the bargain after all.

I glanced up at the sun, wheeling over toward the western horizon, struggled to my feet and began walking on.

It seemed suddenly to be a fool's errand I was on. If Jason Grier and his cronies were indeed heading toward St Joseph or St Louis, they were themselves only a day or two away from the landing on the Missouri River. As early as tomorrow they could find themselves aboard a flatboat or even a paddle-wheeler drifting lazily along the eight hundred miles they would be traveling, in the comfort of a steamboat lounge, smoking cigars and calculating the profit they would be making from their one morning's work.

No matter that Sad Sam and I had spent six months working sunup to sundown for those furs.

Anger kept me plodding on. If it was a fool's errand I was on, I was nevertheless determined to see it through to the bitter end.

Darkness came early. The thick pines around me

closed out every memory of the day. The pine needles were soft underfoot. With each step the scent of crushed pine rose. The needles did not so much cushion sounds as smother them. I was as silent in my passing as a drifting cloud.

Which is why, early that evening, I was able to come up upon their camp before they had an inkling that I was nearby.

The first one I saw seemed to be sleeping on the ground near a cold fire ring, but he had no blanket thrown over him even in the chill of night, and I frowned. The second man was sitting propped up against the rough trunk of a big pine tree. His face was so pale that it was nearly translucent. It was like I could see his skull through his flesh, he was that pale. He was holding a big Colt revolver loosely on his lap, and he tried to lift it as I entered the tiny camp, but either he changed his mind or simply hadn't the strength left to do it.

I strode toward him; it was obvious now that he was badly hurt. And now it was evident that the other man curled up on the cold ground was already dead. I crouched down beside him.

'What happened here, friend?'

His mouth opened, but he had trouble forming his words. When they finally did come, they trickled out like sand spilling from between his lips so that I had to bend nearer to hear him.

'They wanted our horses . . . bunch of men with a cart loaded with furs. . . . Said their mule had broken down. Big men. . . . Harv there,' he said nodding at the

17

dead man, 'was too quick to draw his gun . . . I was too slow.'

Jason Grier and his thugs. It had to be. Their mule had broken down . . . poor old Bess, I thought. Doubtlessly they pushed her too hard trying to get away from the scene of the robbery. 'Where were they heading?' I asked.

'I heard them talk about a ferry landing . . . I don't know.' The old man coughed and blood came from his mouth. I remained crouched down beside him, all the time knowing there was nothing I could do for him. A bony hand stretched out and gripped my forearm with amazing strength and the wounded man's fevered eyes met mine.

He told me, 'At the first sight of the outlaws I sent them into the woods . . . you'll find them there, hiding. They've got two horses.' He paused, took a gasping breath and said, 'You've got to get them to the Diamond.'

Where? Take who there? The man made no sense. Not that it mattered. I was taking no one anywhere. What I was going to do was dog Jason Grier's tracks and deliver justice to him and his band of killers.

'Do it for me, mister,' the dying man continued, more weakly still. 'It was the last promise I made their grandmother. Tell them that Art Faver tried. . . . They're just kids. . . .'

Kids? 'There are two little kids out there in the forest?' I asked. Faver's eyes had closed and I shook his shoulder, trying to rouse him, but it did no good. He was dead. I stood, looking around me with a heavy sigh.

18

My breath frosted out against the night. I was shivering despite my wolfskin coat. I was wasting time; I had to follow Grier now. He couldn't be that far ahead of me.

Just kids. I knew they couldn't survive out here by themselves. I was going to have a tough time fending for myself. I looked around for the wheel ruts marking Grier's trail, found them and halted in my tracks. Clamping my jaw, I turned back toward the camp, feeling like a fool, and called out softly.

'If you can hear me, come on in now. The bad men are gone.'

Nothing. There was no sound at all in the wilderness but the wind whispering through the high reaches of the pines.

'Anyone out there!' I tried a little louder, my voice echoing across the stillness. Had they gotten themselves lost? Run away? I had half-convinced myself that I could do nothing about it anyway, that I had tried, that what needed to be done was to hunt down Jason Grier. What did I care about two lost children. . . ?

What had Sad Sam cared about me?

The thought was shameful. Sam had undoubtedly had another life planned, one that didn't include raising an orphan brat, me. He could have turned his back on me or palmed me off on the first farm woman he ran across, but he didn't. He cared for me and raised me, raised me better than to be the sort of man who would turn his back on two lost, frightened children.

Unhappily I started searching the dark woods as Jason Grier and his wagonload of stolen furs steadily distanced themselves from me.

19

I called loudly and then softly, wound my way deep into the pines and then circled back toward the camp again, thinking they might have heeded my first call to return. I found nothing, heard not a peep.

Standing in the clearing, wondering if there were any way I could scrape a grave for the dead, I heard a tentative childish voice say:

'We're over here.'

I turned toward the voice and saw the three-foot high silhouette of someone. It was a girl. She had her hands clasped behind her back. Her lip was trembling, her starlit eyes wide and fearful.

'What are you doing, Amy!' an incensed boy, a foot taller, a few years older than the girl asked, stepping from behind a tree. 'I told you not to answer him.'

'I'm cold, Tag, and I'm scared,' the girl said in a trembling voice.

'We don't even know who he is!' the boy answered. 'He might be one of them. The killers.'

'I'm not,' I answered. I crouched down and put my arms out to the girl, but neither of them took a step forward. I needed to get them away from the camp, away from the dead. I needed to get them to trust me. I could think of nothing else to say but, 'Let's be on our way to the Diamond, shall we?'

'You know where it is?' the boy asked in astonishment.

'Doesn't everybody?' I replied.

'How far is it?' the little girl wanted to know. She had crept forward a few steps from the shadows of the trees and now I saw a thin, blond-haired tyke of eight or so, dressed in a blue calico dress and laced boots. There was anguish and hope mingled in her expression.

'Not far,' I said with a smile as if I had any idea what I was talking about. 'We'd better get started right now.'

'I haven't had any sleep,' the girl complained.

'You don't want to sleep here, do you, Amy?' the boy said.

'N . . . No, I don't suppose so,' Amy answered.

'All right, then,' her brother said, adopting a manly tone. 'It's time we got started – put some miles behind us.'

'You're right,' I agreed. 'Come here, Amy, I'll carry you.'

She didn't move toward my arms, but stood wearing a small frown. The boy spoke up as if revealing a deep secret. 'We've got horses,' he told me, and my own heart lifted.

'Where? How many?'

'The two of them – ours. Bitterroot, he's mine, and Amy's little Daisy.' He lifted a pointing finger. 'We hid them over there in the brush.'

'Let's have a look,' I said. I stopped to snatch up a blanket lying beside one of the dead men. The night was growing bitter cold; we would need all the warmth we could manufacture.

The horses, when we found them were a mismatched pair. Bitterroot was a stocky bay horse, perhaps eight or nine years old with a patient look about him. The other, Daisy, was little more than a pony. Fawn-colored with a speckled rump, it was the right size for a child of Amy's age, and little use for much else

21

especially along a wilderness trail. No matter – it was what we had, and that was that.

'The two of you get up on Daisy,' I ordered to Tag's dismay. 'I'll have to ride Bitterroot.'

'I wouldn't be seen on that pony,' Tag said angrily.

'Well, no one's going to see you,' I answered. 'Besides, if you don't do that, one of us is going to have to walk and it won't be me.' My voice was gruff but I had pity on both of the youngsters, robbed now of their peace and sense of security, riding with a stranger in the far country.

'I'll do it, but I won't like it.' Tag swung aboard and waited while I lifted Amy up behind him. The girl was trembling with the residue of fear and with the chill of the night. I wrapped the blanket around her shoulders.

'This smells awful,' she complained. It did. It smelled of smoke and man sweat and . . . faintly, of blood.

I swung aboard the indifferent Bitterroot and we started on up an unknown forest trail as the moon sank and faded in the west and the night grew even colder and darker.

The woods thinned as the trail wound its way southward. Now there were occasional cedar trees standing among the ranks of pines and the forest canopy was thinned enough so that we could see the brilliant, cold stars. Tag who had been riding Daisy silently, his sister clinging to him, now reined up with a childish snarl.

'Wake up, will ya?' he demanded of Amy and the boy looked at me with pleading eyes. 'She's fallen asleep twice on me. I had to grab her arm to keep her from falling off.'

Amy rubbed her eyes and looked at me sheepishly. 'Pass her over, Tag,' I said. 'I'll keep her on in front of me.'

We managed the exchange and soon had Amy seated on Bitterroot's neck. She shivered beneath her blanket and I pulled her closer, wrapping the flaps of my wolfskin coat around her. After a minute she complained.

'Your coat smells worse than the blanket!'

I supposed it did. Two years earlier a pair of prowling wolves had gotten into the horse pen where we kept Santana and Ben. Sam had shot and killed the pair of them and I had skinned them out, sewing their hides onto burlap backing. I knew of no way to clean furs, so the coat stank of two years' work, of my sweat, and unbelievably still carried some of the musky scent of the wolves themselves.

'Sorry,' I said and made to remove the folds of the coat from Amy. Two small hands stretched out and grabbed the flaps.

'I didn't say I didn't want it!' she whined. I smiled.

'A little spoiled, aren't you?' I asked. Tag glanced at me and said protectively:

'She's just tired.'

'I know it,' I said.

Our horses plodded on, their hoofs striking the soft earth, making the only sounds in the night.

'How far do you think to the Diamond?' Tag asked me.

'I have no idea,' I finally admitted. Amy, dozing,

23

sagged in my arm. 'Where is it supposed to be?'

'I thought you . . .' Tag was incensed. 'You said you knew where it was!'

'I didn't want to start a long conversation back there,' I told him. True; all I had wanted to do was get the kids, and myself, away from the bloody camp. 'I don't even know what Diamond is,' I said and Tag's face expressed pitying disbelief.

'It's one of Wyoming's biggest ranches,' he told me proudly. 'You can ask anyone.'

'I could, except I've never been to Wyoming,' I said.

His voice held some hesitancy, 'Well, don't you think we're nearly there? Grant – he's the man you talked to at the camp – told me we were just about out of Montana yesterday.'

'He'd have known more about that than I do,' I answered. 'We could have crossed into Wyoming without knowing it.'

'All right, then,' Tag said as if he had made his point. 'Diamond is a little north and west of Sheridan. We can't miss it.' He looked around with new interest. 'We could be on Diamond land already and not even know it.'

I agreed with him and then fell silent as the miles passed. Sometime after midnight the trees fell away enough for us to see that ahead of us lay long prairie, heavy with tall grass and only scattered standing frees. I heard Tag say:

'If that's not cattle country, I never saw any.'

He was right there, of course, and so I made no answer. I kept studying the horizon, east and west, looking for anything that might indicate we were riding near civilization. I saw no structure, no glow of a fire in the night across all of the dark, starlit country.

And then I did.

'Look, Tag,' I said, pointing westward toward a low grassy knoll with a few dozen pines growing on it like spiky hairs. 'There's a building over there.'

'It doesn't look like much,' he said doubtfully.

'We don't need much,' I replied. 'But Amy is dead to the world and I don't feel much more alert.' And the stocky bay horse I rode, Bitterroot, was just about done in. No wonder. He had been ridden all day and now used long into the night. 'We'd better see what we have here,' I said.

We had to dip down into a ragged vale and ascend the outcropping at its head, seeing no other way to approach the building. When we did achieve flat ground again, we found a squat log cabin with a shingle roof, standing alone and apparently unused in the clearing.

'Someone's cabin?' Tag asked.

'I think it's a line shack,' I said. 'It looks like you were right about this being cattle country.' That seemed to excite Tag and he swung down eagerly, more quickly than I could, encumbered by Amy's sleeping form. There was no one around, that was obvious. The windows were shuttered and these were all fastened. I took it for a line shack, a place for cowhands to sleep when they were far from the home ranch. Tag, at the door of the shack whooped softly with excitement.

'What is it?' I asked. He was standing at the rough

door to the building, his finger tapping an emblem that had been burned into the wood there. It looked like, and proved to be, made with a branding iron. The brand was a diamond.

'I knew it,' Tag said. 'I knew we were on my ranch!'

His ranch? I shifted Amy in my arms and carried her to the door which Tag had already managed to shoulder open. The interior was coal black and I fished a match from my pocket, thumbing it to life so that by its feeble flickering glow, Tag was able to spy a lamp sitting on a rough plank table.

By the glow of the lantern I was able to look the place over. There were two bunkbeds along one wall, a rough stove of stones and iron plate, a lopsided cupboard. In the corner was a pile of discarded bits of harness, a torn shirt and one boot. I unrolled the thin mattress on one of the lower bunks and carefully lay Amy down. She murmured, but did not wake up. It was cold in the shack and so we built a fire in the stove with the scattered collection of firewood that had been left behind. It seemed no one had been out to this part of the range for quite a while.

'I sure am hungry,' Tag said and I nodded. My stomach was complaining too. Opening the cupboard I found a pot and a dozen tins of beans. I opened up two of the tins with my skinning knife and emptied the contents into the pot, placing it on the sheet iron griddle to heat. Tag had seated himself at the table, unbuttoning his coat. He was smaller than I had thought, his brown eyes seeming larger in the lamplight. There was concern in them a boy his age

26

should not have to be carrying. I put two tin plates and a pair of tarnished forks on the table and sat down facing Tag.

'Happy to be home?' I asked. I had pulled off my scarf and was attempting to polish my fork with it. Tag did the same, using his shirt tail. He looked at me blankly and then smiled shyly.

'Oh, *home*. I didn't know what you meant.'

'You said that the Diamond belonged to you.'

'It does!' Tag said earnestly. 'Me and Amy, that is. Except – well, we've never seen it.'

'Oh,' I responded, waiting for him to go on. He was thoughtful for a long minute and then began to tell me his tale while I stood stirring the beans which were beginning to heat in their bubbling juice.

'Our parents left the Diamond to us,' Tag began confidently, then his boyish face darkened with remembered sorrow. He sniffed once and went on. 'They both died, you see. Funny, that. They went back to Illinois to bury my grandmother. . . .' Again he hesitated and when he continued, his voice broke as he told me, 'A runaway team pulling a freight wagon hit them as they were crossing the street. It was—'

'That's all right, Tag,' I said. 'I don't need to hear any more.'

'I don't mind,' he said. He folded his hands together on the table and worked them against each other. 'Mother and Dad were going to bring us west finally. We had been staying with Grandmother, you see. Dad said the Wyoming country was no place for children. But then they had gotten a good start on the Diamond,

27

built a house and barn, and they decided it was time to bring us – me and Amy – back home, especially since Grandmother. . . .'

The kids had had a tough time of it, losing their grandmother and both parents. On top of everything else their escorts had been shot down on the trail. It was a wonder that Tag was standing up to the telling as well as he was. I tried to inject some liveliness into the conversation.

'So now you've returned a prosperous ranch owner?'

'I suppose,' he said doubtfully. Then, 'Sure, that's what I am!'

'Who's been running the ranch?'

'My aunt and uncle,' he told me. 'Dad's sister and brother. I don't really remember them.'

'I'm sure they're good people,' I said although, of course, I had no idea what sort they might be.

'Well,' Tag decided, 'Amy and me will have a home, and a finer one than most. Think of all the orphans who haven't even a scrap of bread!'

'You're right,' I agreed. 'I was almost one of those myself.' I went on to tell him about my life, about my parents' deaths and Sad Sam. He listened intently, watching me through the hazy light cast by the smoky lantern, seeming to draw a small measure of comfort from knowing that he and I had suffered similar misfortunes.

'And those men, the ones who killed Harv and Art Faver back at the camp, they were the ones who also killed Sad Sam?' he asked when I had finished.

'So it seems, yes.'

He shook his head in wonder. His demeanor toward me had changed noticeably. Our shared troubles had drawn us nearer. We might have been brothers in his eyes. And for now we were thinking the same way. The boy glanced once toward the door as I collected the plates from the table then returned his eyes to me.

'I see that you barred the door,' he commented. 'So you saw him too, did you, Brian?'

'Yes,' I answered. 'I saw the man following us, too.'

THREE

The sun, when it broke, was low and hard, giving off red light through the broken clouds but little heat. The slanting sunlight caused a jewel-like glow to bounce off the morning dew. In the hollows, still deep in shadow, there was rime underfoot where the horses, their nostrils steaming, left circular imprints with their hoofs. We continued southward, me still holding Amy as I guided Bitterroot along the trail toward Diamond.

I saw no cattle on all the vast expanse of grassland, and that puzzled me. If Tag also noticed this, he made no comment. He continued to watch the backtrail, looking for the man who had been following us the night before. I could not see the man either, although if he kept to the higher slopes, the timber would continue to hide him.

Amy, who had complained at length about the breakfast of canned beans she had had to eat, became more restless. She chatted cheerfully as we rode, but squirmed so much in my arms that finally Tag offered:

'I'll take her for a while, Brian.'

Gratefully I handed her over to her brother. Amy

released my coat reluctantly and was still pouting when we started on again, she riding behind Tag on Daisy.

'I wonder how far the house is,' Tag said. I could only shrug an answer. I had no way of knowing. How big was the Diamond? A few hundred acres? A few thousand? Tag had said that it was one of the largest ranches in Wyoming; if true it would be quite large. Many thousands of acres.

The breeze began to grow as the sun rose higher, turning yellow, and it shifted the manes and tails of our horses, chilling us through our coats. As the day progressed the temperature plummeted, and finally on the northern horizon we saw the beginnings of what I had dreaded all along: great stacked thunderheads, black against the crystal blue sky towered over the mountains, promising bad weather. It would snow and snow hard. If only it would hold off until we could find the Diamond Ranch house, or failing that, other shelter. I had no wish to be caught on the open plains with two children in the midst of a north country blizzard. The wind rose and the skies darkened. The land began to lift again and grow more wooded. Now there were oaks scattered among the pine trees, swaying barren and leafless before the sweep of the wind. Tag rode with his shoulders hunched; Amy was barely visible wrapped tightly in her striped blanket. The snow began to fall.

Wind-driven, the flakes struck against my eyes and stung my cheeks. I squinted against the weather and continued to guide the stolid Bitterroot through the trees, keeping the wind at our backs as a crude compass. Tag said something, but when I glanced at him his teeth were chattering so badly that I could not make out what he was saying. I knew we were in for a bad time if the snow continued, and the storm showed no sign of weakening. Along the high peaks black clouds snaked through the pines vengefully. The earth was in shadow and the wind whistled through the forest, snapping off weaker high branches, showering us with pine cones. I could not stop my shivering; my wolfskins were not enough to cut the chill of the flurries.

Then I saw, or thought I saw through the tumult of the storm, beyond the dark ranks of the pines, a structure huddled in the valley ahead of us. I lifted a pointing finger, but Tag had already seen it and with a glance at me, he heeled Daisy on. The little pony had little more speed to offer, but she charged gamely on down the slope toward what we could now see was a wide-spreading ranch house.

Diamond, I thought. It had to be, didn't it? I was unjustifiably proud of myself for having delivered the children home. More, the thought of a warm fire and walls to block the cut of the wind cheered me as we approached the house. Smoke rose from a stone chimney at the log house's center, but the wind whipped the dark smoke away before it could rise and plume. Probably half of the smoke was being thrust back down the chimney into the house itself. No matter – that would be a small inconvenience to us compared to the harsh weather we had ridden through. The snow had lowered, thickened and was now roiling past us as we guided our ponies toward the house.

Tag was young, but even this eleven-year old boy knew enough to guide our horses toward a nearby barn. The animals would be taken care of first. Inside the carelessly built barn, we dismounted, limbs stiff with the cold. I helped Amy from her pony's back and she sighed and looked up at me with a weak smile.

'That was getting to be a close one,' she said, and I thought, for a nine-year old she was pretty brave. Two good youngsters, I decided, as I unsaddled Bitterroot and backed him into a stall and watched Tag, his sister helping as best she could, stabling Daisy.

Together they stood at the barn door, studying the dark form of the ranch house through the swirl and surge of the storm. They seemed suddenly confused, reluctant to proceed. I put on my best smile, walked between them and put an arm around each.

'Ready?' I asked and their heads bobbed silently. I led them once again into the teeth of the storm to march across the empty yard where already snow was drifted against the base of the oak trees there, and together we stamped up onto the porch of the big house.

I rapped on the heavy door with my knuckles. Beside me Amy shivered in her tightly wrapped blanket. Tag had his hands thrust into his pockets as far as they could go. His hunched shoulders were nearly to his ears. I rapped again, harder. The door opened.

A tall, dark eyed man in range clothes, a belted revolver at his waist peered out, frowned at me, taking in my round badger fur hat and wolfskin coat and demanded:

'Who are you and what do you want?'

'Shelter,' I said. 'And I've brought two cold children who need the same.'

'Just a minute,' the unfriendly man said. He shut the door, but left it ajar a few inches and I could hear words being exchanged inside the house. In another minute a woman with pale blue eyes, her blond hair knotted at the back of her head, opened the door wide. She too was wearing range clothes – jeans and a red flannel shirt – and she looked down at the children and said:

'For goodness sake! Get inside, you three. What was Cole thinking leaving you outside in this weather!'

The children were hustled inside, Tag with some reluctance at having a woman's arm placed around him. Inside across a plank floor I could see two men standing in front of a large native stone fireplace with an arched hearth. One of them was the dark eyed, mean-looking man the lady had called Cole. The other man was pale-haired like the woman who had ushered us inside. Both held a white mug of steaming coffee.

We dripped water on the floor as we were guided toward the fire. As I had guessed, smoke drifted back into the room, but it was not unpleasant. The fire was of cedar wood and the scent was fragrant. More, the room was *warm.* I already had the urge to shed my coat and hat, but waited until invited to do so.

'I am,' Tag said like a little gentleman, 'Tag Bellows, and this is my sister Amy. Also, allow me to introduce our travelling companion, Mr Brian McCulloch.' It was said in an adult manner, and I considered that I had again underestimated the maturity of the eleven-year old. Someone in his background had given him a good deal of polish.

'Tag?' The woman looked from one child to the other with wonder. 'And Amy! Don't you recognize me? Aunt Bettina, and that is your Uncle Grant. Has it been that long since we've seen you!' Bewildered, she asked, 'But where are your mother and father? Where are Peter and Rose?'

I waited, looking away as Tag again painfully recounted his parents' fate. The blond man, Grant Bellows, his eyes concerned, listened closely. Cole's lips were tight; he stared at the fire, one shiny boot propped up on a brass fire dog.

'Terrible, terrible,' Bettina Bellows said. She crouched now to take Tag's hand and to look into the eyes of Amy. 'Don't worry now, you're home.'

'I'm plenty hungry,' Amy said. 'He only gave me beans to eat,' she added, nodding at me. Bettina glanced at me and then laughed.

'You'll have a good solid breakfast. First, though we're going to see that you bathe!' And the kids were a sight after the long days on the trail west. Tag's clothes were next to rags and Amy's hair was tangled, her face smudged. As for me – well, I guess I never looked much better anyway. Standing there in my mountain gear: wolfskin coat, round badger-fur hat on my head, my fox-skin leggings, I must have looked pretty primitive to these lowland folks.

'What about Brian?' Tag asked. 'Does he have to bathe too?'

'Probably be a new experience for him,' Cole

sneered, increasing my dislike for him, but Bettina answered firmly.

'We'll let Mr McCulloch get started on his breakfast while you two clean up.'

'He needs new clothes too,' Amy said, 'his stink!'

'Well . . .' Bettina said, flushing slightly. 'We'll see what we can do about that – if he wants to change clothes. Cole? You probably have clothes that would fit Mr McCulloch.' Cole nodded.

'I guess I might,' he answered, but his tone indicated that he had no intention of loaning me any to wear.

'I'll dig up something,' Grant Bellows said. 'I'm sure I've at least got a shirt and an old pair of jeans.'

'That's settled then,' Bettina Bellows said, standing, wiping back a loose strand of blond hair from her forehead. 'I'll have Laurel start some water boiling for your tubs. And have her set a place at the table for Mr McCulloch. Laurel! Where are you?'

'Here, Miss Bettina,' I heard, and a tall, dark woman entered the room from a side door. The scent of cooking drifted into the room with her.

'We need some water for the children's baths. Do you remember Tag and Amy, Laurel?'

Tag immediately rushed to Laurel, seeming to have a stronger memory of her than he did of his own aunt and uncle. As far as that went, she was a memorable-looking woman. Tall, slender, graceful in her movements. Her eyes were as black as obsidian, but gave off warmth. She crouched, clasped Tag to her aproned breast and smiled at Amy, stretching out a hand toward the girl. Without reluctance Amy also went to her and Laurel led them away presumably toward their baths.

Before she had gone, Bettina called after her, 'Laurel, set a plate for Mr McCulloch, will you? It seems that he is the children's savior.'

As soon as the door closed behind Laurel and the kids, Cole stepped toward me and asked savagely, 'How'd you come to find the kids, McCulloch? In all that wild country?'

His voice was suspicious, angry. Grant Bellows calmed his friend. 'Take it easy, Cole. The man saved the kids, didn't he?'

'I want to know how he happened to come along just when their escorts were gunned down.'

'Sometimes things happen in strange ways,' I said, not wanting to bring up the whole story of how I had been trailing Jason Grier on another matter of business: Sad Sam's murder. Both men waited, but I said no more. Finally Bettina interrupted the cold silence. She touched my elbow and told me:

'Laurel will have hotcakes and bacon going on the griddle soon. And there's coffee ready.'

I nodded my thanks and followed the gesture Bettina made toward the kitchen door. Inside I found myself in a long white-plastered room with two plank tables and flanking benches and two iron stoves, one of which was lit. A pot of coffee and a white ceramic cup had been placed on the table. Laurel was busy with the children, it seemed. I peeled off my wolfskins, ashamed of that coat of mine for the first time, removed my round badger-skin hat and seated myself within arms' length of the coffeepot.

After a minute Laurel returned, but she only glanced at me before putting two big black kettles filled with water onto the stove. I poured myself a cup of coffee and sat there alone as Laurel breezed back out, going into a hallway that led to somewhere in the back of the house.

The coffee was dark and hot. I sipped at it, feeling my bones warm as the heat of the kitchen comforted me. Beyond a single high, narrow window I could see the storm shifting and blowing. Large flakes pasted themselves against the glass pane and then were melted to slide away by the heat of the kitchen. I pondered my situation.

I was in a place I was not wanted. At least by the man named Cole, although Grant Bellows seemed nearly as suspicious of me, and Bettina Bellows' welcome hadn't been exactly warm. Well, I couldn't blame them a lot. A stranger, dressed in north mountain-country furs knocking at their door with two children and what seemed a wild story about finding them in the wilderness. Maybe they thought I was trying to extort payment from them. Maybe they thought that I had done the killing myself.

My mouth tightened at the thought, although it didn't matter what they thought. I did not care in the slightest. I had brought the children home. Now I was free to go on my own way.

Wherever that was.

How could I hope to catch up with Grier now? We were in the middle of a blizzard, and I hadn't even a horse or a minimum of supplies. I frowned and lifted the coffee cup to my lips just as Laurel entered the room again. She looked my way.

'What's that frown for? Just a minute and I'll have your food ready.'

'Need help?' I asked as she hoisted one of the big iron kettles containing hot bath water, using a hand towel for a hotpad.

'I'll manage it,' she said with a faint smile. 'I'm used to doing the heavy lifting around here.'

I studied her as she fussed with the pots, turned and went out again, opening the door with her toe. She was younger than I had first thought, my age or a little older – around twenty. Lithe, but certainly strong. Her face was cheerful now that she was working . . . and away from Cole and the Bellows. There was some sort of unhappy undercurrent here, but I had no need to understand it and didn't waste my time pondering all of the possibilities.

I simply drank my coffee and before I had finished my second cup, Laurel had returned again and started flapjacks frying, with bacon sizzling in a second pan. It was a comfortable place to be, in this warm kitchen, watching a woman perform these small tasks for me. It was too bad it would have to end almost before it had begun. I moved my elbows so that Laurel could serve my breakfast and reflected briefly on what Sad Sam would say if he could see me sitting here, in what was a castle compared to our sagging cabin in the mountains, piping hot food before me. I thought I knew:

'Quit gawking at that girl and stuff your gullet! That's

liable to be your last hot meal for a long, long time.'

As I was finishing up my breakfast, Tag returned to the kitchen, his face scrubbed, hair slicked back. He was followed by Amy who sort of flounced in, doing a little dance, holding her skirt up as she went to Laurel's side. Laurel, stirring up a fresh batch of hotcake batter, glanced down and smiled.

I said to Tag, 'Well, you made it home.' I didn't get the sort of cheerful response I was expecting.

'To the ranch,' he replied glumly. I supposed he was thinking that Diamond was not really home without his mother and father, and started to say something along those lines when he looked at me sharply and said, 'Something's up around here, and I don't like it.'

Tag had that expression again, the one where he looked far too old for his years, too concerned with the world's troubles. His sister prattled on to Laurel about something. Finally I asked:

'What's troubling you, Tag?'

Instead of answering, he said, 'Will you stay on for a while, Brian? I know you've got places to go but . . . in this weather you won't get far anyway, will you?'

'I don't suppose so, no,' I had to agree. 'But why, Tag?'

'I'd just feel better that way,' he said. Then he looked up and smiled as Laurel delivered a tall stack of hotcakes and homemade brown sugar syrup to the table. Tag was engrossed in his eating, no longer in the mood for conversation, and so I rose.

'Is there any of that hot water left?' I asked Laurel. She looked me up and down and told me:

'I can boil some more. You want to take a bath, too?'

'Yes, I'd like to,' I answered without confessing that I could barely remember the last time I had had a real bath and it would seem like heaven to me to soak in warm water. Maybe she understood all of that without me saying a word. She was a woman who seemed to know much. Maybe she could tell me what Tag was upset about. I would ask her later.

For now I followed her down the short hall to the bathroom. There was a small entry room with a wooden chair and glass mirror and beyond it the actual bath. The porcelain tub was still damp from the kids' scrubbing. A few damp towels lay scattered on the floor.

'I'll clean this mess up for you,' Laurel offered, starting to collect the towels, but I stopped her.

'I can handle that, I think. You're already doing enough.'

She nodded her thanks and scuttled away again. I wondered, as I stepped into the tiny bathroom and began discarding my furs, who Laurel was and how she had come to be on the Diamond. I stood in my twill trousers and long john shirt waiting for Laurel to return with some hot water. I picked up the towels and placed them over the back of the chair in the other room to dry. Waiting there, I thought I heard someone hailing the house from out of the storm. Curious, I stood on tiptoes to peer out the high window. Past the snowflakes obscuring the glass I saw movement.

I squinted, wiping at the window fog with the back of my hand. A rider was approaching on a dark horse. He paused in the yard, not swinging down. I could not

41

make him out clearly, but saw that he was dark, wore a black hat and that his mount was a spotted pony. Someone from inside the house, bulky in a thick coat, strode to where he waited. The two men had a brief conversation, and then the horseman started his pony away at a walk. I thought the man he had met was Cole, but he kept his back to me and before I could make certain, Laurel came through the door with a huge iron kettle. Struggling through the doorway she upended it into the tub, spilling steaming hot water into the bath.

'One more trip,' she said with a weary smile, and I nodded, waiting while she returned to the kitchen for more water. I looked out the window again, but saw only the snow falling through the black oaks of the ranch yard. Mentally shrugging, I sat down on the chair, waiting for Laurel to return so that I could begin my bath.

When she had come and gone again, I lowered myself gratefully into the tub. I soaked and scrubbed until the water was cool and then stepped out, toweling myself hard enough to rub the skin off. Stepping into the entry room I saw that someone had placed a blue flannel shirt and a faded pair of black jeans on the chair. My furs were missing.

Dressing, I heard a tap on the door. When I opened it Tag stood there holding a pair of cowboy boots. 'I got these for you,' he said, handing them over. 'I had to guess at the size.'

'Where are my own clothes?' I asked, knowing that I would be traveling on again soon, and in the winter cold my own garments, as shabby as they might seem, were more suited to my journey than ranch garb.

'I think Laurel said something about airing them out. Brian, no offense, but you were kind of gamy-smelling.'

I tried the boots, tugged them on and found that they fit surprisingly well. Old, scuffed, but useable. All I needed now was a Stetson. And a shave.

'You look good in those,' Tag said as I stood. 'Have you ever been a cowboy?'

'Only for a short time,' I admitted. 'Two summers ago Sam and I were hard up for survival money and we took a job on a Montana ranch – the Cable, if you've ever heard of it. I did my share of roping and branding, though I had a lot to learn from the old-time hands.'

I should have been surprised, but was not, to spot the closed razor resting on a fresh small towel in front of the mirror.

'You people have decided to scrub me all the way down, haven't you?'

'To see the new you,' Tag said. With a little grin he added, 'It was all Laurel's idea.' Then his worried frown returned and as he watched me soap my beard, he asked, 'Did you see him, too, Brian?'

'Who do you mean?' I asked, stropping the razor. I studied the boy's worried face in the mirror.

'The rider. The one who just arrived. I saw him heading toward the bunk house. The man with the spotted horse. He's the one who was following us back down the trail.'

FOUR

I did feel like a new man when I strode once more into the living room of the ranch house. I was warm, stomach filled, bathed and shaved. Cole was gone, but Grant Bellows still stood near the fire, only now he was holding a glass of what seemed to be whiskey in his hand. Bettina sat on one of the gold-colored settees in the room, working at her embroidery. She glanced up as I entered the room and commented:

'Who is this stranger, Grant? Did you invite one of your friends over without telling me?'

'He does look better with a little polishing, doesn't he?' Grant responded. 'You've eaten, have you, McCulloch? Come on with me, then, we'll have to find you a place in the bunkhouse where you can hole up until the storm blows over.

I nodded my thanks. It was obvious that neither of them had more they wished to say to me, and I had nothing to talk to them about. From a closet Grant removed a gray hat and a well-worn sheepskin-lined, leather jacket and handed them to me. I had a feeling that the items had once belonged to his brother, Peter

Bellows. I shrugged into the coat, planted the hat on my head, and followed Grant out of the warmth of the house.

The wind was still gusting; snow still fell in a heavy blanket as we trudged across the short distance to the squat bunkhouse. Grant halted at the steps leading to the door of the building as if it were beneath him to enter the place, and said, 'Go on in and have someone introduce you around.'

I pushed on through the door to the inside of the long log building. I let in a gust of cold wind and the men there, six or seven of them, glanced my way with irritation or simple curiosity. In the center of the room flanked by rough hewn bunk beds was a round cast-iron stove. A scrawny older fellow with tufts of salt and pepper whiskers and jawline which indicated he had lost a few teeth crouched on his heels, prodding the fire.

I walked the length of the bunkhouse. Those who continued to watch me, studied me curiously. I knew this was because I had no gear with me, nothing but my Colt. I had noticed the damp footprints right away.

They were drying quickly in the heated room, but still there was a trail of prints leading to the man who sat a lower bunk in the far corner, eyes flickering to me and then shuttling away. This, then was the man who had talked to Cole in the snow-blanketed yard only minutes before. He was dark, lean but not thin, and there was a scar running all across his forehead. I pretended not to notice him, but my eyes must have already given me away, the way he avoided my gaze.

'Where'd you blow in from?' a friendly voice asked as I passed another bunk. I looked to see a heavy-built cowboy lying on his bunk, hands behind his head. He had gray eyes, a nose with some prominence and a high shelf of bony brow. All in all he had a dangerous look about him, but he was smiling now as he watched me.

'Down from Montana,' I told him, and a few men, no longer curious, nodded as if I had told them something they already knew.

'Well, Montana,' the man on the bunk said. 'Pick yourself a bed and sit down to wait. Like we all are, for the snow to stop falling.'

'Are all of these beds empty?' I asked, indicating three in a row that had their thin mattresses rolled up.

'They are. The men who were using them are down on the south line now, watching the big herd. My name's Szabo, by the way,' he said without offering his hand. 'That dried up critter over by the fire is Mr Thomas Terkel. Known as Turkey.'

'You leave me alone, Szabo!' the little man said, but he was grinning toothlessly. 'The man's always picking on me.'

'You deserve it,' Szabo said. 'That there,' he told me, pointing toward a kid with a wild mop of shaggy curly hair, 'is "Curly" Sledge, I don't know why they call him that. And that's Gordon Blaine over in the back looking at nobody. The rest ... well, you boys introduce yourselves. I was just getting ready to dream about Little Nell down in Cheyenne. With any luck I'll see her at the end of the trail.'

'I heard she married a preacher and had a pair of

twins,' the old man named Turkey said and Szabo laughed.

'Maybe, maybe she did, but I'll bet she's still working in the Wingate Saloon.'

'You said we were going to drive these cattle?' I said, stunned by the prospect. 'In this weather?' A cattle drive at this time of year was virtually unheard of in the north country. And why? Most ranches like Diamond would have culled their herds in the spring, sold off in the summer and be settling in to ride out the winter storms.

'That's what the boss says,' Szabo answered. 'Me, I don't ask questions. The herd's being held about five miles south, and when the weather clears, we're going to Cheyenne. That's what Cole says, so that's what we're doing.'

This was something I could not have planned on. I did not have to involve myself, of course, but I was at the whim and will of Diamond Ranch just now. I had not so much as a horse to call my own, and they certainly wouldn't want me just lounging around the ranch while others worked a difficult job.

After rolling out the mattress, I sagged onto the bunk I had chosen. Briefly I thought of my lost horse, Santana, and damned Jason Grier for taking that fine sorrel of mine. Then as I began to inwardly rage at the knowledge that Grier and his gang were far beyond my reach by now, I stretched out on the bunk and stared at the ceiling, sparing only a single glance for the man called Blaine, wondering still about his secret meeting with Cole, still suspicious that he was the man who both

Tag and I had seen following us from the spot where Harv and Art Faver had been killed by Grier and his gang.

Sometime in the middle of the afternoon the storm broke and some of the men went outside just to look up at the clearing skies. When a lingering storm hovers across the land like this one had, it sometimes seems that there will never be blue skies again. The men in tall boots and hats stood around in front of the bunkhouse, some of them smoking. Others leaned back against the logs of the barracks wall and just let the new sun touch them. It was still cold, very cold, but the mood was of shared warmth. When a flight of doves was spotted winging their way homeward across a gap in the ragged broken clouds, a couple of men actually cheered.

It seemed they were already tired of winter and winter had hardly begun.

I found a wooden bench on the sunny side of the bunkhouse, brushed away the snow lingering there and sat down. After a minute the man, Szabo, joined me. His dark face reflected unhappiness. He, it seemed was not sharing in the communal good spirits. As he settled, crossed his legs and placed his hat carefully on one knee, he spoke.

'Looks like we'll be leaving soon now that the storm's broken.'

'For Laramie?'

'That's right. They've pushed the railroad line that far west. Laramie's a trailhead now. We get the chance to try driving a thousand ornery steers south. They won't like moving at all. And there's the chance we'll catch a real blizzard along the way. I can't imagine trying to herd cattle through something like that.'

'Then why move them?' I asked Szabo. He shrugged his heavy shoulders and grinned.

'The boss wants them moved.'

'I don't know a lot about the cattle business,' I said, 'but isn't a winter drive risky?'

'Oh, it's risky all right, Montana,' Szabo answered. I was going to have to get used to being called 'Montana,' I supposed. 'But there's a chance that many of these steers won't make it through winter on Diamond range. Grass will be snow-covered, water frozen, temperatures down to where neither man nor beast can survive. Simply, Diamond is carrying too many cows for the range.'

'I see,' I said, but I didn't. They should have been aware over this past spring and summer that they had to cull the herd further. Why wait until winter weather threatened to drive the cattle to the railhead?

'I guess Mr Bellows put this off – making the decision to sell the beeves off that is – because his brother was not here.'

'That's not exactly it,' Szabo said. Again his broad, almost brutish face was creased by a smile. 'You say "Mr Bellows". Now, Peter Bellows was a savvy cattleman. He thought that by using sheltered pastures and stocking hay the herd could survive the northern winter and that when spring came he'd have a strong herd. It's Grant Bellows, and more his wife,' Szabo said lowering his voice, 'who want to move the herd and sell it quick. As soon as they found out that Peter and Rose had died, they moved in, bringing Art Cole along with them.

'I don't know where they came from or what they did before, but cattle ranching was not their specialty.' Szabo shrugged. He suddenly smiled as he spotted a hare already wearing its white winter coat dart through the underbrush near where we sat. I asked Szabo:

'Grant Bellows and his wife . . . and Cole . . . they weren't living on Diamond before his brother was killed?'

'No,' Szabo told me. 'I don't think the two brothers got on well together. But once Peter and Rose died, well Grant had the right to do whatever he wished with Diamond.' He paused and spat. 'Even if it's run the ranch into the ground.'

'For fast money.'

Szabo didn't answer that, but his look said it all. I thought I had a sketchy understanding of matters now. Peter Bellows had built Diamond and meant to accept any winter losses, holding his naturally multiplying herd until it flourished. Grant Bellows and Bettina seemed to be hungry for money, immediate money, and were not considering the long-term effect of a sell-off.

And the long-term would impact Tag and Amy. Their legacy was the ranch; now it was being stripped of its assets.

I sat unhappily looking out across the snow-covered land, no longer drawing cheer from the clearing skies. I found myself wondering about Grant and Bettina, about the events that had put them in a position to become immediately wealthy.

I found myself wondering about the accident that

had killed Peter and Rose Bellows.

I found myself worrying about what was being done to Amy and Tag.

None of this was my business. I shouldn't have cared, should have been content to snag a horse and ride out of there, hoping to somehow track down Jason Grier and reclaim what I could of the small fortune he had taken from me back along the trail. St Joseph now seemed impossibly far away.

So did Laramie.

But then, I considered, if I did go along on the cattle drive, I could take a train east from Laramie, maybe reach St Jo not that far behind Grier, who, after his river trip and fur trading, was bound to remain in the big city for a little while at least, enjoying the fruits of his crime.

Getting to my feet, I nodded to Szabo and started toward the big house. I wanted to go along on the drive. I needed to get to the railroad line. Grier and his gang may have considered themselves well away from retribution, but they were far from it.

'Brian!' A voice called and I looked over to see Tag in a leather jacket and knit cap crossing the yard behind the big house to meet me. His face was pink with the cold and carried that too-old look of concern he had. He offered me a smile, however, as we met.

'How are you doing?' I asked, taking his hand which he offered as a man's greeting.

'Oh, I'm all right, Brian, but I don't like Diamond. Isn't that funny? All I could think about when we were staying with Grandmother was that one day the ranch would be built up with a proper house and Mother and

Dad would come and get us and bring us home. Now,' he shook his head, 'I don't know – Diamond is not home.'

He continued as we walked beneath the oak trees which were shedding damp clumps of snow: 'You know all about this winter drive that Uncle Grant and Bettina are excited about?'

'I know something about it,' I replied.

'They say they need the money now to maintain the ranch. My question is: will there even be a ranch to maintain after all of the cattle are gone? How can you have a ranch, Brian, if you don't keep it stocked?'

I had no answer for him. I marveled again at Tag's maturity for an eleven-year old. It was obvious he had done a lot of thinking about the situation.

'Laurel says that the cattle aren't even theirs to sell,' Tag told me. 'She says that Diamond has been put into receivership for me and Amy. I'm not sure what that means.'

'It means an adult is assigned to watch out for your best interests.'

'That's what I thought,' Tag sighed. 'How can they just sell all of our . . . assets,' he asked after hunting for the word.

'I don't know,' I answered, shaking my head. 'It's beyond me, the legal side of things. It just seems they're in an awful hurry to sell those cattle.'

'Aren't they?' Tag asked, stopping to stand facing me in the cold shade of the trees. 'Uncle Grant explained that they didn't want to suffer a winter kill of the herd. But my father was willing to risk it, wasn't he? Maybe

52

there is nothing wrong here, but I know my father was more of a cattleman than Uncle Grant will ever be.'

'About this idea of receivership,' I said. 'What else does Laurel know about the legal matters?'

'I don't know. Not much, I guess. All I know about Laurel is that she can be trusted and she is worried, too.'

'Where did she come from, Tag? She was here, on the ranch, when you were little, wasn't she?'

'Yes. She was a Plains orphan. Her parents couldn't make a go of it out here. Something bad happened. I think it was the Indians that got them, but Laurel doesn't ever talk about it, so that could be wrong. Laurel was just here one day – my mother found her in town and brought her back. They got along well, Mother and Laurel. They used to always laugh in the tiny kitchen in the old house, and. . . .'

His thoughts darkened as newer memories crowded out the old. He asked me abruptly:

'Do you think Grant and Bettina had my parents killed?'

Although I had wondered about that too, I wasn't ready to make a judgement on no evidence. I didn't answer the question. Instead I asked:

'When did your aunt and uncle arrive here?'

'I don't know. Just before Mother and Dad went east to bring Amy and me home. Grant and Bettina needed a place to be, and Father needed someone to watch the ranch. Father let Cole stay here too. Grant and Bettina brought him along with them.' In a lower voice, Tag told me, 'Father didn't like Cole at all. I once overheard him having a private talk with my mother, and he said, 'Cole smells like an outlaw. As soon as we return with the kids, I'll send him packing.'

'A lot of the hands seem to feel that way, too,' I said. 'Do you know Szabo? I don't think he likes Cole.'

'I remember Szabo. Not well, but I recall him. Father trusted him. He, Curly and Turkey have been here since before there was even a bunkhouse built. They had to sleep in a lean-to. Laurel tells me that there are some new men around who are cut different – some of the men with the herd down on the south range. They, she says, are nothing more than thugs. I have the idea that maybe they used to ride with Cole, that they all were a part of a gang and now they're planning the biggest job of their lives – stealing one thousand Diamond cattle.'

'That's a little wild, Tag,' I said, not because I was certain that he was wrong, but to try to calm him.

'Anyway,' Tag said hopefully. 'You'll be able to watch them and make sure that the money from the cattle sale gets back here. I don't care about that money for myself, Brian. I can make it living off the land, but Amy's just a little girl.'

I had no answer for him. I had been drawn into something I knew nothing about and had only a little while ago convinced myself that all I wanted was to reach the railhead and make my way east, to continue my hunt for Jason Grier. Now I looked down into the trusting, hopeful eyes of Tag, put my hand on his shoulder and walked on without admitting any of that.

We entered the house by way of the kitchen door.

There was the warmth, the smell of cooking – a ham was roasting – and Laurel, wiping her hands on her apron, her bright smile in place, eyes welcoming.

'Give you men a chance to wander around and you stay out until you're half-frozen before you rush home to hearth and home, remembering what you've left,' she said, helping Tug out of his jacket.

The scolding was done light-heartedly, and both Tag and I had to smile in response. I seated myself at the table while Tag, summoned by Amy, walked off toward the back, his impatience with his little sister showing.

'He's a fine boy,' I said.

'He is,' Laurel answered without turning to face me.

'Both of them think the world of you, Laurel.'

'Do they?'

We remained silent for a minute while she opened the oven and did something to the ham. I didn't know how to broach the subject, but it was time. 'Laurel,' I said, 'Tag seems to have the idea that they are trying to steal the ranch from under him and Amy. Steal all of the meaningful assets, anyway.'

'Why does he think that?' she asked, facing me as she leaned against the counter, wooden spoon in one of her crossed hands.

'I don't know for sure. Maybe something he heard. Sometimes kids are more alert to the small currents than we are.' I raised my eyes to hers. 'He told me something about there being a conservator for the estate, that Diamond has been placed into receivership so that nothing can be done without his permission, that Grant and Bettina really have no right to sell those cattle.'

'But what can I do about it, Brian?' Laurel asked, and I looked into those black, now troubled eyes, and said:

'It's you, Laurel? You're the kids' conservator?'

'Who else was there? Yes, Brian, I am their legal guardian although they do not know that yet. Nor do their aunt and uncle. You see, before Peter and Rose Bellows left to travel east, they took me with them into Sheridan to see an attorney there. It was, they said, "Just in case, since anything can happen on a long journey". And so I signed all of the papers as they were given to me. It is such a responsibility. Now it seems that those kids are being taken advantage of.'

'Laurel,' I said, 'if I were you, I'd make sure those papers are put away someplace where no one can find them.'

'I've already done that, Brian.' She was obviously deeply troubled. Her face brightened suddenly and she said more confidently, 'It will all work out now. Now that you are going along on the drive to Laramie, you will be able to make sure that the money from the cattle sale is brought back to the children.'

Would I? I wondered. I didn't even know if I was going to make that trek, let alone how Grant Bellows, Cole and their crew would feel about me trying to take charge of the proceeds from the cattle sale.

'I know you will look out for them, Brian,' Laurel said, coming nearer to me. 'You have brought them this far and saved their lives. I know you would not let them down now.'

'It's not a matter of what I want, Laurel . . . but what can I really do?'

'Just stay alert, Brian. Perhaps you can have the money paid in a bank draft payable only to Diamond Ranch in the kids' names.'

'I don't think they'll like that idea much – Grant and Art Cole.'

'Don't forget about Aunt Bettina,' Laurel cautioned me. 'I think that she is the driving force behind this plan. She seems to me to be a very greedy woman.'

'I'll remember that,' I promised. 'What else should I watch out for?'

'Your own life,' Laurel answered casually. 'If they have the faintest idea of what you are up to, Brian, it won't be long before they try to stop you by any means available.'

FIVE

I wasn't feeling all that perky when I left the house despite the fact that Laurel had dished up baked ham and yams for me; I was growing very fond of that woman's cooking. From the front porch of the ranch house I stood looking out at the bedraggled oaks and the cloudy sky, and watched the cold wind trifle with the upper branches of the trees. A red, long-tailed yard dog to whom I had not been formally introduced trotted past, glanced my way and went on. Tag was suddenly at my side.

'What will we do about a horse?' he asked. 'I'd let you take old Bitterroot, but he's had a long journey already. Besides, he's no cutting horse, is he?'

Already Tag had assumed that I would ride to Laramie with the herd to watch out for his and Amy's interests. My heart sank a little as his bright eyes watched mine. I wanted to pull out. I wanted to track down Jason Grier. Yet how could I leave with matters as they stood? I smiled and told Tag everything would work out and after a minute or so he returned to the house since he was coatless and the cold wind still drove across the plains. I had started off the steps when Art Cole emerged from the house. He wore a black hat and black leather coat. He watched me with his hawk eyes and attempted a smile which never reached his eyes. I knew he didn't like me, but it didn't matter.

'I overheard part of your conversation,' he said. 'Enough to know that you are planning on making the trail drive with us and that you need a good horse under you. Well, come on over to the barn,' he said putting a hand on my shoulder. 'I've got an animal for you.'

I didn't feel like going to the barn with Cole. I didn't feel like ever going anywhere with the cunning, scarred man, but I did. What else was I to do? No matter how things worked out, I would be needing a horse.

We crossed the yard where the snow was turning to muddy slush and walked to the barn, Cole always lagging a step behind me.

He remained behind me as we reached the barn door. I didn't like the feeling I was getting, but it had to be done if I was going to get a horse to ride. I stepped into the dark interior of the musty barn and before I had taken two more steps they were on me.

Someone tackled me at the waist and I felt a heavy fist glance off my temple. I went to the ground, writhing and kicking in fury. It didn't slow their assault. The man who had tackled me had rolled off of me at least, and I managed to get to my knees before one of them aimed a kick at my head. I moved my skull fractionally as the boot struck my flesh. Instead of stunning me as intended, the kick merely tore a deep gash in my cheek.

Hot blood flowed instantly down my face and into my mouth.

I rolled aside, taking another glancing kick on my ribcage, and came up against a stall partition. The horses along the length of the barn were now rearing up, kicking at their stalls and whinnying with wild-eyed excitement.

I grabbed the edge of the partition and got to my feet as the three men formed up around me. They were wearing bandanas tied around their faces, and in the shadows I could not make out who they were. I was only sure that I had not seen two of them before. They were big men, bulkier than anyone I had yet met on the ranch and thicker than even the heavy-shouldered Szabo.

They approached methodically again, fists bunched menacingly, and I looked helplessly toward the doorway. Cole, of course, was gone and there was no one else arriving to aid me. I had never been in a real fist fight. I had once gotten into a brawl with a scrawny ranch hand up on the Cable Ranch, but we were pretty evenly matched and our fight consisted more of clutching, elbowing and rolling in the dust before it was broken up by some of the other hands than anything else.

This fight was not going to be broken up. These men had more in mind than roughing me up.

I locked eyes with one of the men, feinted right and then darted to my left, circling the wild-eyed roan horse stabled there. I had seen what I wanted leaning against the stall and now as the men yelled threats at me, I took it in my hands.

The barn was dark, but even in the dimness they could see the glimmer of light on the tines of the pitchfork I held. They didn't like it a bit. One of them backed away, growling. He started to reach for his gun, but the man in the middle stopped him. Apparently they wanted no shooting here, not with so many men in the nearby bunkhouse.

We stood fixed for a long minute. I had the pitchfork held low. My hair was in my eyes; blood continued to trickle down my face. They inched into positions they gauged to be better for resuming their assault and I saw one of them tense as he prepared to launch himself at me.

When the barn door was flung open cold sunlight flooded the interior. Two men stood in the doorway. Szabo, who muttered a curse and started forward, and Curly Sledge at his side. Szabo seemed ready to brawl with the men, but Curly had slicked his Colt from its holster and the ratcheting of the hammer mechanism was loud in the silence of the barn.

My three attackers took to their heels, racing toward the small side door. Curly aimed his pistol at them but lowered it again. Szabo chased them for a few steps and then halted as the three men slipped out into the yard. In moments we could hear their horses being ridden hard away from us. I placed the pitchfork against the stall and leaned against the partition as Szabo and Curly came up to me.

'What started that?' Curly asked.

'I have no idea.'

Szabo had pulled his neckerchief off of his thick neck and now dabbed at my cheek carefully, examining it. 'You'll probably need a few stitches,' was his assessment.

Curly was still curious.

'Wonder what they wanted,' he said. Curly tilted his hat back on his head, holstering his Colt. 'Did you know them?'

'No. I have no idea. . . .' I was interrupted by Art Cole who had come in and was now walking innocently toward us.

'Some of the boys playing rough?' Cole asked. He did not smile, but neither did he look surprised. Why would he be? I had no doubt that he had steered me this way to be beaten. I wanted to accuse him, to have it out then and there, but there was no profit to be made from antagonizing Diamond's foreman. I only asked him:

'Which horse were you going to let me have?'

He showed me a deep-chested gray with a white blaze. I noticed that he was one of the few horses that had not gotten overly excited at the man-fight. Calm, strong looking, around six-years old, I took an immediate liking to the horse. I was also given tack, a cast-off saddle and bridle, and considered that the freedom a pony offered was nearly payment enough for the beating I had taken. Now I could make plans for my own future.

The sun was sinking toward the far mountains as Szabo, Curly and I made our way back across the yard toward the bunkhouse. The wind had fallen, but the temperature was dropping again. The red mud that had been underfoot now was rapidly freezing.

'That's a good horse you got,' Szabo said, keeping his dark eyes fixed forward.

'I think so,' I agreed

He told me, 'It belonged to Peter Bellows.'

In one way that dulled the pleasure I had had accepting the big gray horse. I didn't want Tag to watch me riding his father's pony, expecting me to see him through his troubles like a father. I thought of the disappointment the kid would suffer if his last image of me was me riding away on my own quest for vengeance rather than taking care of Diamond Ranch's business.

Why did I ever have to meet up with Jason Grier!

In the bunkhouse Turkey saw to my wound as well as he could. As I sat on my bunk, he dabbed carbolic on the cut and then, squinting and muttering to himself, the whiskered old man set to work running stitches through the flesh on my cheek. I tried to put my thoughts elsewhere, to concentrate on anything but the cold bite of the steel needle. It didn't do a bit of good. It hurt.

My head hurt, my cheek hurt, I felt beat up from one end to the other. I was tired, too tired to get up to join the others for supper, too over-tired to sleep. I had noticed that Blaine, the man who had been trailing me and the kids across the miles, was absent from his bunk. Had he been the third man, the smaller man, in the barn? And if so, what could he have against me?

I forced all of my worries, all of my questions out of my mind. I vowed that I would sleep one night without worries. I had nearly sunk into the soft folds of sleep when the men returned from their meal. I opened one eye to peer at Curly who was shaking his head worriedly. He had begun packing his poke sack with a clean shirt and socks.

'What is it, Curly?' I asked him.

'We're pulling out at daybreak. Pushing those steers to Laramie.'

'If it snows. . . ?

'If it snows, if it rains, if it shines or the wind threatens to blow us away. The boss wants those cattle on the move at first light.'

I fell asleep again somehow. It seemed like only minutes later that someone was shaking my shoulder, trying to rouse me. 'Get up,' Turkey said. 'Time to go to work.'

I sat up, yawning. That automatic movement caused my cheek to hurt and I put a hand to my burning jaw. There was only the low red glow from the iron stove to light the bunkhouse in the pre-dawn hour. No one else was rising from his bunk. Sitting on the edge of the bed, I asked Turkey:

'What do you need me for?'

He was slipping into a ragged old coat that fell to his knees. 'You, me, Sylvester got to finish loading up the chuck wagon. Get your boots and coat on then meet us in back of the kitchen over at the big house.'

'All right,' I agreed. Dressing as quietly as I could, I made my way across the dim interior of the bunkhouse to the front door. Opening it I let a gust of frigid wind in and I slipped out the door, closing it firmly behind me. Tugging my coat collar up, pulling my hat low, I trudged across the snow-laced yard toward the kitchen where a lantern burned in the window, illuminating the covered chuck wagon pulled up in front of the door. A younger ranch hand I had met only briefly greeted me. He was wearing gloves and a woolen scarf. 'Sylvester?' I asked, a little embarrassed that I could not recall his name.

'That's right. And you're Montana?' His face seemed boyish beneath his wide black hat, and he had an easy, gap-toothed smile. We shook hands and Sylvester led me to the rear of the wagon. Turkey was inside the kitchen. I could hear voices there – his, Grant Bellows' and Laurel's.

'This won't take long,' Sylvester promised as he thrust his gloved hands into his armpits and stood shivering in the wind. 'Most of the stuff is loaded – tack, medicine, blankets, flour and beans. The rest is stuff we're moving from the kitchen pantry. It shouldn't take more than an hour.'

'How'd you get stuck with this job?' I asked, my teeth chattering a little as I stared at the star-cluttered sky.

'You and me – we're the two newest hands,' Sylvester told me. 'The other boys need their rest. It's going to be a hard day's work for them, trying to rouse and start those steers. Besides,' he added, 'I'm driving the chuck wagon, and I was up harnessing the horses, checking the wheels and hubs, brake and axle. This is going to be a long drive and I can't have the wagon breaking down under me.'

'What about Turkey? Is he going with us?'

'No!' Sylvester laughed. 'He told me they were keeping him on the home ranch where he will have a bed and stove every night. Says he finally found some benefit to getting old.'

As Sylvester said that, the back door to the kitchen opened. I did not see Grant Bellows, but Laurel was there, energetically stacking items from the pantry – a few sides of bacon, and crates of tinned goods among them – and Turkey who stood watching, tallying the items on a scrap of paper.

'Looks like we can start loading,' Sylvester said.

It was better to be moving than standing still in the cold and so we went to the kitchen door where a waft of tantalizing warm air drifted out from the cook stoves within. Laurel looked at me, started to smile and then returned to her work, saying nothing. She wore a close-fitting dress of a sort of reddish-brown color with a lot of buttons up the back that suited her. Behind Laurel, in the door to the hallway stood Tag, watching us unhappily. After carrying one load of goods out to the wagon, I returned and took a minute to approach Tag.

'Why so glum?' I asked him.

'I want to go along. I told Uncle Grant that, but he said no. I'll bet I could drive the chuck wagon as well as Sylvester!'

'Maybe,' I agreed, trying to speak soothingly, 'but you're still at the age where you've got to be told what to do and accept it. This is going to be a long and dangerous trail, Tag.'

He looked at me but didn't answer. He turned away and went to his room to pout as I watched. I felt

Laurel's hand fall softly, unexpectedly on my shoulder.

'Is he angry with you, too, now?' she asked.

'I guess so. He really wanted to go along on the drive.'

'He's so young. And he's still tired from the long trail home. Grant was right in this case,' she said, 'though I hate to admit that that man is ever right about anything.' We were standing close together and I could smell the scent of a fresh bath on her, a sort of lingering lilac smell. I wanted to say something but was not sure how. Turkey's crackling voice brought me out of my reverie.

'Are you going to give us a hand here or not, Montana!'

I nodded, shouldered a sack of potatoes, picked up a black iron kettle and carried them both out into the cold, handing them up to Sylvester who was waiting on the tailgate of the wagon.

While we waited for Turkey to finish his tally, Sylvester and I sat there on the wagon. He nodded at my cheek and said, 'Got into a little scrape yesterday, did you?'

'Yes, I did.' I explained briefly about the fight and about Curly and Szabo arriving to break it up.

'I'll bet those boys scattered quick enough when they saw Curly pull his Colt.'

Frowning, I considered that. Yes, they had, although they outnumbered him three to one. 'They did,' I answered.

'Then they know Curly,' Sylvester said with a nod.

'Is Curly good with a gun?'

'I never seen anybody better. I don't know where Curly ever drifted in from, but you can bet he's seen some fighting in his time. How about you?' he asked, indicating my own holstered pistol. 'Are you any good with that?'

'I really haven't had the practice,' I admitted. 'Maybe Curly can give me some tips.'

'Maybe,' Sylvester said carefully, 'but I think it takes more than a few tips to make a gunfighter.'

'I guess you're right,' I answered. Turkey emerged from the kitchen, closing the door behind him. I could see Laurel at the window, and I hoped that she was looking for me. I put that thought out of my mind; it did no good to think of such things.

'How about Szabo?' I asked Sylvester as we slipped to the ground from the wagon tailgate. 'Is he that good with a gun, too?'

'Szabo? No, no I guess he isn't. But those boys who attacked you would have known Szabo too, and if they knew him well enough, they'd have known that he could take them apart an arm and a leg at a time with his bare hands. You were just lucky, Montana, that it was those two who happened along while you were getting beaten.'

Laurel caught up with me before I started away for the barn to get my horse. She stepped near and gave me a small package. 'Ham sandwiches,' she said. Her words frosted from her lips in the cold. Her eyes were intent.

'Thanks,' I mumbled.

'It's nothing. After all, we orphans have to watch out for each other, don't we? You, me, Tag and little Amy.'

68

'You're talking about making sure that the kids end up with the money from the cattle sale,' I said.

'I only want you to *try* to make sure that's the way things work out!' Laurel said, studying my face so intently that I had to turn my eyes away, because I didn't even know if I would do that much once I had a horse between my legs. I had other thoughts about that in my mind. *Jason Grier.*

'Tag is counting on you,' Laurel said, touching my shoulder lightly. 'And so am I.'

By the time I had saddled my gray horse and joined the other ranch hands outside the barn the sun was rising, spreading a golden glow across the snowfields, lighting the high reaches of the trees with morning fire. Grant Bellows and Art Cole sat their ponies side by side, Grant appeared agitated as he looked at the men and then toward the rising sun.

'We're already losing time,' I heard him say to no one. And within minutes he had us riding away, turned toward the south and the waiting herd.

When we reached the south range, the sun was splashing the scattered islands of snow with crimson light. Closer to the pine trees that circled the open range I could see the herd. There were a thousand or so of them, red- and white-backed steers the tips of their horns gleaming in the sun. To my mind there were just too many of them to be handled by the number of men we had. I said something like that to Szabo who had chosen to ride beside me.

He said, 'Charles Goodnight pushed a herd of nearly

two thousand longhorns out of Texas up to the Kansas railhead when he only had eighteen men riding for him. We won't have but around eight hundred steers now that the yearlings and two-year-olds have been culled out, they being too young to travel that distance, and it's not just us to do the work; most of the Diamond hands – men you haven't met – have been down here watching the beeves we pushed from the north range last week.'

I nodded my understanding. The north range which both Tag and I had noticed was without cattle, had been swept clear of them by other Diamond cowboys. By Szabo's reckoning there were around twenty of us to push the cattle on down to Laramie. To me, eyeing the milling steers, it still didn't seem half enough, but Szabo was consoling.

'It's not that far, Montana. If it doesn't snow,' he added, glancing over his shoulder at the northern skies which for now still held clear. 'And old Charlie Goodnight, he had more than just his longhorns to worry about. They had to make that drive through Comanche country.'

'We don't have that to worry about,' I said, trying to buoy my own spirits.

'Of course not,' Szabo said, laughing. He leaned out of his saddle to slap my back. 'The Indians are too smart to come out in a blizzard after us.'

I smiled, but I knew that what he said was true. I also knew, as we all did, that the storm we had suffered through was only to be the first of many pushing down from Canada at this time of year. I had spent brutal

70

winters shacked up in Montana before. The storms I had seen . . . well, no one was going to drive cattle through that kind of weather.

But we were about to try it.

That was the reason Grant Bellows was in such a hurry – the weather. He knew that we had only a matter of days, maybe only hours, before the next big storm hit, and we had to be on our way with these half-trail-broken steers before the icy weather killed them or snowdrifts blocked our passage, before the hard-blowing north wind blasted against us with such ferocity that a man would not even be able to see his horse's ears, let alone work cattle.

'It'll be a big payday for the Diamond cowboys,' I said. Curly had drifted up beside us on his little appaloosa pony. He replied dourly:

'For those of us who make it through alive.'

'Don't spook Montana, Curly,' Szabo said with a laugh that I felt was superficial. 'This is nothing. A cakewalk.'

I held my horse back a little as Szabo and Curly rode ahead. I knew then that Szabo had only been laughing with me to try to brighten my spirits. He was as deeply troubled as Curly seemed to be. As every man who would be riding with this herd had the right to be.

We started from the Diamond in the winter of that year pushing a herd of balky steers toward Laramie. Around us the cattle lowed and complained and among us rode men who meant me harm.

SIX

I drew the drag position, which in the dry lands to the south was considered the worst assignment and given to the new men who were compelled to eat dust from the herd the day long. Here, in the mid-winter mud and patched snow, it was still a test. The steers grew obstinate, unwilling to leave their familiar haunts where they had shelter from the blustering wind and plenty of stocked hay. Either Art Cole or Grant Bellows had planned the first leg of the drive so that the herd passed through a confining gray notch in the low surrounding hills, keeping the herd pinched together and leaving them little room to bolt. Riding drag, however, I along with Szabo and two brothers named Collier, had our hands full with those cattle who were determined to stay on home range and simply turned their tails to the direction of the herd and tried to bolt back toward home range.

There was slush underfoot, especially after the hoofs of a thousand steers had passed over the ground, and it would have been comical to an disinterested viewer to watch us as we tried to guide our slipping horses in our wild efforts to contain the scrambling, wild-eyed steers. Comical if you weren't among the flailing hoofs and slashing horns of the panicked cattle.

Szabo and his pony were remarkable in their combination of balance and firm resolve. The gray horse and I were less successful. The gray, whose name I learned was Traveler after Robert E. Lee's favorite mount was more of a parade horse than a cutter; even so the animal was better than I at anticipating the twists and lunges of the renegade cattle. We came within inches of being gored or, worse, trampled half a dozen times in the first few miles, and these were my fault more than Traveler's.

As the hours rolled by most of these would-be defectors began to accept the inevitable and that, along with their herding instinct kept them in line as the herd flowed up through the rocky, snow-mortared crags and into the long canyon connecting us with the open land beyond flowing toward Laramie.

I was sweating beneath my sheepskin coat and in my hat. The perspiration froze when the fingers of the icy wind touched it, and my legs began to ache from the simple effort of holding the saddle, my arms from the repeated task of hieing the steers with my lariat. It had been a long time since I had done this sort of work, and even then I had not been a skilled cowhand. I found myself watching the sun, hoping for a noon break.

But Cole and Bellows were determined to push on. Each mile gained was a mile toward their financial goal, and the weariness of their crew was the last thought in their minds.

'Are we going to stop?' I asked breathlessly as Szabo, nudging a reluctant red steer back into the herd's trailing edge came alongside me.

The big man smiled and tugged his hat lower. 'I doubt it. The idea is to push and push hard, Montana. What's the matter – does this make you feel like you'd rather be back trapping beaver?'

'Yes,' I managed to pant. 'Yes it does.'

At least in the high mountains, although we worked from first light to last, a man simply rested when he was tired. It only made sense. And few of our prey, if you did not include the wolves and occasional bear, were bent on attacking us, which seemed to be what these recalcitrant cattle had in mind.

'You'll be all right,' Szabo said, his nearly-brutish features hardening. 'The first days are necessarily short, and we'll bed them down as soon as we clear the pass. It'll be coming dark by then. A good meal and a night's rest and you'll be ready for morning.' I tried to take comfort in his words, slogging along endlessly in the mud left in the wake of the cattle.

And then it began to snow.

Hard.

The storm came blustering in from the north like a sprawling angry giant. The sky went briefly to pitch black as the wind gusted fiercely, and then the snow fell and the world went white. I was lost in an impenetrable veil of snow. I could see no farther than Traveler's nose. Even the men riding beside me vanished, only occasionally appearing as dark shadows against the background of turbulent white. The temperature must have plunged thirty degrees in thirty minutes. I shivered as I rode, bent low to try to avoid some of the wind's thrust. I found myself wishing for my Montana furs.

As for the cattle – they had disappeared as if a vast blanket had been thrown over them all. I could hear them lowing, their horns clicking each other's as they moved more closely together as the storm raged. I could feel their heat and smell them, but only now and then did they appear – a rust colored mound of hair and muscle and bone, a wild brown eye gleaming in the near-darkness.

And what would happen when night did fall? This was insane; we could not go on.

I sensed rather than saw Szabo ease his stubby buckskin horse up next to me.

'The boss says to keep them moving!' he shouted with a voice muted by the bellow of the wind, although he was straining at the top of his lungs to be heard.

'That's insane!' I shouted back. I don't know if Szabo heard me or not, but he drew his horse away, vanishing into the white turbulence.

How could we continue in this weather? I was no cattleman, but it seemed to me that the only prudent thing to do was to halt the herd and bunch them as best we could until this blew over. Otherwise, we risked losing them all as they scattered and sought shelter. Now we were out of the long notch in the hills and the wind was even fiercer, and as the land spread out the cattle were bound to wander. They were still unused to the trail and we were incapable of keeping them bunched.

Why keep them moving? Obviously Cole and Grant Bellows wanted this drive to end. They wanted to reach Laramie as soon as possible, and were willing to accept their losses if we arrived with only half the herd. A quick payday for them; a huge loss for Diamond.

Some more sensible mind prevailed an hour or so on and I found myself among a bunch of cattle slowed by the halting of the herd ahead of us. I drew back from them and waited. Finally through the whirl and bluster of the snowfall I saw someone – Curly I think, although I could not even make out his appaloosa pony's distinctive markings – hold up an arm and circle it in the air, meaning we were to bunch the steers – those that could be seen in the wash of snow.

Blessedly, the storm eased slightly just before dusk, and I saw the pale, flickering light of a campfire burning. I hadn't been given an assignment for the evening, and so I took it on my own to guide Traveler toward the fire which illuminated the vague silhouette of the chuck wagon. I swung down stiffly. My joints were locked with the cold. I felt battered and my extremities half-frozen. If I had a nose or ears left on my head, I couldn't feel them. I walked toward the welcoming, wind-twisted fire, leading Traveler. Billy, the younger of the Collier brothers had been assigned to the role of wrangler and he emerged from out of the storm, offering to take charge of my horse. I turned him away. I would feed and see to Traveler myself. The position we were in was terrifying as it was. I didn't want to consider how it would be for a man without a horse caught in a Wyoming blizzard.

I found Sylvester, his hat tied down around his ears with his long woolen scarf, and he only gestured toward the gallon coffee pot. No one had the breath to waste in speaking unnecessarily. Holding Traveler's reins I scooted as near to the fire as possible and hunkered down on my heels. I didn't feel like such a fool when I saw that many of the older, more experienced riders had kept their horses with them as well.

There was no conversation at all. We sat like ghosts around the flickering campfire, passing a tin plate containing salt biscuits among ourselves as we drank the coffee before it could freeze in our cups. The fire did brighten the night, but it did little to warm us. I crouched, shivering violently as I tried to chew one of the cold biscuits.

A hand touched my shoulder and I glanced up to see Curly crooking a finger. I rose and he shouted above the raging wind:

'You and I've got first night herd shift.'

'All right,' I said wearily, although I had no idea how we were supposed to successfully control the cattle – those that we could see. The hours passed and the wind alleviated somewhat. The snow continued to fall, but in heavy clumps, not like the swirling whey of the day. Once I actually saw a hopeful star among the clutter of clouds as Traveler and I circled what I could see of the herd, moving through two feet of new snow. The horse had been fed, of course, from the scant supply of hay the wagon carried, but Traveler was as weary and as cold as I.

Curly and I had worked out a crude routine which

saved us unnecessary struggling. We rode in opposite directions around the herd and when we met we continued on, using the trail that the other had broken, so that after an hour or so we had a rough trail trampled into the snow which made it easier to follow and kept us from wandering away from the herd accidentally. The cattle themselves seemed calm. Perhaps they were too exhausted or cold to be rambunctious. For the most part they stood together, using each other's body heat, and lifted mournful eyes at me as I passed. Steam rose from their reddish backs as snow constantly fell on their bodies. I had never felt so sorry for animals before.

I met up with Curly as we finished one more circuit of the herd at about ten o'clock that night.

'It's about time someone was relieving us, isn't it?' I asked through weather-split lips.

'You'd think so,' he answered. 'Can you even see the camp?'

'No. Maybe that's it. They can't even find us!' I said with a laugh.

'Could be,' Curly answered with a tight smile. Then I heard the close report of a gun and Curly looked at me with astonishment and pitched forward from the back of his startled appaloosa. As the pony danced away, Curly fell to the earth, hot blood from a nasty wound to his throat staining the pure white of the snow.

I kicked out of my stirrups and hit the ground rolling, pawing at the handle of the Colt riding on my hip beneath the flap of the sheepskin coat I was wearing.

I came up on one knee and saw a muzzle flash, clear in the night – angry red and yellow and I fired back wildly, throwing myself flat. For only a moment the storm curtain parted and I saw the man, recognized his horse, and as he wheeled away I snatched for Traveler's reins to give chase.

I hit the saddle and heeled the gray horse, and we fell into pursuit through the surge and foment of the storm. My quarry did not turn and fire as he rode, but he somehow kept gaining ground on me until at last he vanished into the white tapestry of the blizzard and I could no longer even follow his horse's tracks.

I drew up Traveler who shuddered as I pulled him to a stop. I stroked his quivering neck and sat staring into the still blankness of the white night, having lost any chance I had at tracking the killer on this stormy night. All I could do was recover Curly's body and take it back to the camp. He could not be buried in this weather, of course. We would probably have to wrap him blankets and carry him along to Laramie in the wagon.

Traveler trudged on through the hock-deep snow as heavier flakes continued to fall. I had not been cautious enough; I had underestimated my enemy. For a few hundred yards from the herd I felt Traveler stagger, stiffen and only then heard the echo of a heavy-caliber rifle. I kicked out of the saddle as Traveler rolled to the snow and lay pawing at the air in a death run.

I lay still, hand clenching the grips of my Colt, behind the fallen horse. He was still now, the night silent. I could see nothing, no one, but I continued to stare out at the snowscape surrounding me until my eyes ached and seemed blistered from the cold. No one came. Night swirled past and finally I rose, disoriented and suffering bitterly in the cold. The marksman had missed me, but he had done worse. He had left me stranded in the night blizzard with no way to reach my camp and crew. No one was going to find me, come to my rescue. I sat against Traveler's unmoving form, using his body's warmth as a defense against the cold, his bulk as a partial shelter from the cutting wind. I sat and I waited, my Colt clutched desperately in my hand.

Morning brought sunlight. When I opened my eyes the glare off the snow was as blinding as the storm's darkness had been. I had to move, however, and now was the time to start while there was light and clear weather.

It was still stunningly cold and so I removed Traveler's saddle-blanket, slit it with my skinning knife and wore it as a poncho. The saddle itself I had no more use for than Traveler did.

I started on, squinting into the glare of the new day, trying to retrace my tracks to where we had been first attacked. I could not see the herd which bothered me, but then I was not sure how far I had ridden in pursuit the night before, and the herd had probably been started southward again at first light. There were no tracks remaining in the two-foot deep snow after the night's storm, and no real landmarks on the open prairie. Taking my bearings from the sun I staggered on, wading through the snow.

From a low knoll I peered southward, eastward, but

still I could see no trace of the herd. If they had started at first light, they could have been pushed to the horizon by now – Grant Bellows was in that much of a hurry to reach Laramie. The only surprise was that I did not find dead cattle, exhausted from being pushed to the limit of endurance and beyond.

I glanced northward constantly as I walked. There were stacks of black thunderheads looming over the mountain tops; it would snow again and I needed to find shelter, even the crudest sort to weather the night in if I could not catch up with the herd. And that looked more and more unlikely as the sun rose high overhead, glittering off the mantle of snow which stretched out southward toward eternity . . . or at least as far as Laramie.

The wind still blew roughly and it seemed warmer than when I had risen. I needed to rest, but there was no place to halt. I was hungry, but that could not be helped and so I simply ignored my stomach's complaint. My legs were a different matter. They ached with the constant effort of treading through the deep snow. My chest burned, my vision began to swim. It was a wonder I saw the bit of red, the shadowy figure of a man moving nearly parallel with my route on the opposite side of a snowy hummock. I thought I recognized him by his bulk, and scrambled madly up the snowbank to shout down at him.

'Szabo!'

He paused, looking around as if his mind were playing tricks on him, as if the ghosts of Wyoming were summoning him. I tried again.

'Szabo! It's Montana! I'm up here.'

His head turned toward me and I waved frantically. I saw recognition on his dark face and I half ran, half slid down the opposite side of the hummock to find the big man standing there, wiping his face with his red bandana. He blinked at me curiously and then smiled, placing a heavy hand on my shoulder.

'Hello, kid,' he said. 'What are you doing out here?'

Briefly I told him, as we started on our uncertain way across the snowfields. 'I thought that maybe they'd send someone out to try to find me. They were bound to run across Curly's body and wonder where I was.'

'Send someone out in that blizzard?' Szabo shook his head heavily. 'Not likely; no one could have found you, and any searcher would be lucky to find his own way back to camp out in that storm. Besides, do you think Art Cole or Grant Bellows would care enough about you to look?'

'No,' I answered. 'Just the opposite. They wanted me gone enough to send someone out to kill me.'

'But it was Curly—' Szabo objected.

'We were sitting our horses together, talking after we'd made a circuit of the herd. They got Curly, but it was me they were trying to kill, I'm sure of that.'

'It makes sense,' Szabo said, plodding his way heavily on, steam issuing from his thick lips. 'There was no reason for anyone to kill Curly. I'd like to know who the low dog was that did the shooting!'

I told him, 'I saw him, Szabo, well enough to identify him. It was Blaine who did the shooting.'

'Gordon Blaine!' Szabo halted in his tracks to gawk

at me. 'What could Gordie Blaine have against you?'

'Nothing personal,' I said, 'but Blaine works for his bosses. I suppose you noticed that he hadn't been around Diamond for a long time.'

'Sure. He told us that he left Diamond to try his hand at prospecting, gave it up and came back.'

'Did he tell you that he was following the kids and me all along the trail?'

'Blaine? Why?'

'I have a few ideas. This isn't imagination, Szabo. Tag and I both recognized Blaine and his horse.'

'But I don't see—' Szabo's broad face showed bafflement.

'I think he was tracking the kids all along, waiting for his chance. They had two bodyguards with them, however. A man named Faver and another called Harv. They'd been escorting the kids back to Diamond. While Gordon Blaine bided his time Harv and Faver were killed by men known to me. Blaine couldn't have been happy when I appeared out of nowhere to shepherd the kids.'

'You can't mean that you think Blaine meant to harm the children!' Szabo said in amazement. The hard-bitten cowhand was obviously shocked by the idea. 'But why!'

'Diamond,' I said simply. 'And don't forget that Peter and Rose Bellows are dead, Szabo. I'm not so convinced that their deaths were accidental.'

'I don't understand all of this, Montana. Fill me in,' said Szabo at last. 'Tell me the whole story – what you know, what you suspect.' He looked ahead across the long plain. 'It's looks like I've got the time to listen.'

I told him all that I knew and all that I thought I knew as we slogged on. He listened silently, wonderingly. When I was through he just wagged his head heavily from side to side. Much of what I had told him he did not wish to believe, but he could see that it all fit together too well to be ignored. It seemed that Bettina and Grant Bellows had moved onto Diamond, taken stock of matters there and decided that they could use the ranch to bankroll their lives. Peter and Rose's departure had given them the opportunity they had been waiting for. If the two could meet with some sort of an accident far away from the ranch – say being hit by a runaway wagon – the ranch and all of its assets would fall into their hands.

Except that the children would be in the way. Surely Peter and Rose had made provisions for their children. Well, that was easily cleared up; a lot could happen to people traveling the long trail, and if Tag and Amy did not make it back to Diamond, the ranch would fall to the ownership of Peter's brother and sister.

Szabo didn't like listening to it any more than I liked telling it. I was wondering how he happened to find himself afoot, and as we walked on he told me: 'It was the darndest thing, Montana. When I woke up just before dawn I was rolled up in my blankets, feeling stiff and groggy. My head ached terribly. Someone had hit me over the head while I was asleep. I tried to move, to sit up, and found out that someone had tied my ankles and wrists while I slept. Someone had hog-tied me and just left me there to freeze to death.'

'It figures in a way,' I said. 'Curly was out of the way, by accident or design. I was away from the camp. Turkey is back at the ranch . . . that is, all of the old hands loyal to Peter Bellows, anyone who might be asking questions about the kids' inheritance after the cattle were sold, was gone. Grant and Bettina could do what they liked. The new-hired men either know nothing of the situation or they are men Cole brought in because they had no loyalty to anyone but him and a fat payday.

'They would have made sure that you had an accident somewhere along the way, Szabo, and Curly as well. I'm sure of that.'

'In the light of what you've told me I'm almost sure myself,' Szabo said with a heavy, vastly disappointed sigh. 'If I found anyone trying to hurt those kids . . . but what can we do now, Montana?'

'Just what we're doing,' I answered. 'Because I mean to catch up with Grant Bellows in Laramie before he can make a run for it with money that should belong to Tag and Amy.' Szabo gave that sad, heavy nod again. He was wondering if we had a chance of reaching Laramie before Bellows and Art Cole had concluded their business. So was I, but that was what we intended to try.

We plodded on, the wind still increasing at our backs, the thunderclouds creeping toward us from the far mountains to shadow the earth with their dark threat.

SEVEN

We began to pass dozens of dead cattle lying in the snow. It made my heart sick to see them. More, it made me angry knowing that they were strewn across the plains like the dwindling resources of the orphans, Tag and Amy.

Szabo muttered, 'Look at all that steak, and me half starved to death.' I knew that he was only trying a joke to avoid showing his true feelings. 'What a waste,' Szabo said as we passed another dead steer. 'Why did Grant Bellows have to get in such a rush to deliver the herd to Laramie?'

'He didn't have a choice,' I replied. 'Once the children returned, he had to act fast before some judge interfered and men with badges showed up on Diamond to serve him with cease and desist papers. He knew he had no right to sell these steers, but he was determined not to let the opportunity pass him by.'

'A judge?' Szabo asked, glancing at me. He wiped the back of his face where the dark whiskers were growing heavier now.

'Sure,' I told him. 'As soon as travel around here

grew easier, the conservator was bound to contact a judge and inform him of what Grant Bellows obviously had in mind – stripping the Diamond of its resources.'

'A conservator?' Szabo said thoughtfully. 'I guess there must be one. Peter and Rose wouldn't have left things up to chance. They were a thoughtful pair. Who is it?'

I hesitated. 'I'm not sure if it's my place to say.'

'Must be Laurel,' he decided instantly. 'Who else could it be?'

I didn't answer. We trudged on through the snow, passing many more animal carcasses; Grant Bellows was rapidly thinning his profit, although I knew there would be plenty of money to be made off the cattle who survived this mad drive south.

Some time in mid-afternoon the going got too difficult for me. My slashed cheek had begun to ache again, my legs felt like they were stuck in cement. The cold wind blew and the dark clouds were again shadowing the wide land. All in all, I reflected, I would have preferred being locked up with Sad Sam in that snowbound mountain cabin. Even that would have made for a more pleasant winter. Finally I felt that I could take no more.

'I've got to rest soon,' I told Szabo as I stopped, hands on my hips and breathed in the cold air deeply. 'I can't go on much longer.'

'You can,' he said positively, and I looked at him to see that he was smiling faintly and that he had his finger upraised, pointing toward the southern horizon. I could see low, dark forms, maybe a dozen of them, their rooftops white with snow and my heart leaped.

'Laramie?' I asked in disbelief.

'Or someplace near it. What do you say we keep on walking?'

We did so. The going was no easier, but now that we were in sight of our goal, my determination easily overwhelmed my fatigue. It was growing dark and the snowfields had turned purple by the strange light of the dying sun when we staggered into civilization.

By the time we reached Laramie it was very late and snowing again. The first few buildings that we had seen were a small settlement whose name I never knew – if it even had one. It wasn't much of a place, but a local fanner and his wife took us in out of the cold and served us cornbread and soup. Receiving directions, we walked on, feeling better about our chances. However, the farmer had been far off in his estimate of how far Laramie lay ahead of us and we trudged on wearily through the night and the new snowfall until midnight.

'Now what?' Szabo asked as we stood in the center of a rutted street that was half mud, half ice. The big man was hugging himself tightly, stamping his feet to try to keep warm.

'Shelter,' I said. 'Anywhere at all.' Bellows could wait until morning. That herd of cattle was not just going to be there one minute and magically transported the next. Even if Bellows had a buyer lined up, still the cattle would have to counted, examined and paid for and a train would have to be ready to take them east.

Of course if Grant Bellows had simply taken the money and run, we would have a problem finding him but at least some of the crew would be in town. No sane man was going to be willing to ride off into a new storm following the cattle drive they had just completed. Someone would know where Bellows and Art Cole were. For now, however, Szabo and I needed warmth and sleep.

We stumbled upon a rickety old stable. If anyone was around, we didn't see him, and we didn't wait around to ask permission to sleep there. We simply made a pile of loose straw in the corner of the last stall and crawled in. It was still mighty cold – the wind whistled through the cracks in the plank wall – but we were better off than we had been in a long while, and I managed to fall off into a deep sleep, awakened only occasionally by the chill in my bones or Szabo's deep-throated muttering.

The man who woke us wasn't rough about it. I peered up from my sleep-encrusted eyes to see a man about as thin as the rake he was leaning on. His lined face did not smile, but there was no malice in his watery blue eyes. Beyond him I could see a wide stable door open to the day. White clouds scudded along across a bright blue sky.

'You boys aren't supposed to be sleeping in here,' the stablehand told us in a cracked voice. His tone indicated that he had said this to many men, many times. 'Did you sneak your horses in as well?'

'We don't have any horses,' I said. Szabo was sitting up heavily, rubbing at his head where he had been slugged. 'We walked in.'

'Through that storm?' the stablehand said, frowning. 'You must've wanted to reach Laramie pretty bad.'

'It was more that we wanted to get away from where we were,' I said.

'No horses . . . and I don't suppose you have any money either?' he asked us. Looking from me to Szabo.

'I've got two silver dollars,' Szabo admitted, touching his pocket, 'but I was sort of hoping to use them to purchase something to put in my stomach.'

'Keep what you have,' the stableman said. 'I'm supposed to ask that question, you understand. The man who owns this stable doesn't want the place turning into some sort of cheap hotel. Me, I make about a dollar a day working here. I know all about being broke. But I'll have to ask you to clear out before the boss gets here.'

Szabo and I rose stiffly and slipped out the side door through which we had entered. The weather was cold with scattered clouds as we made our way along the muddy, snow-patched streets looking for a place to eat. As we walked I kept my eyes moving constantly, watching every man we passed, each rider. Laramie was large, larger than I had thought and larger than any town I had yet seen, but if Bellows, Art Cole or any of the crew were around, it was a good bet that they would be on one of the main streets. A stranger in a town usually hunts along these thoroughfares looking for his comforts, being unfamiliar with out of the way shops and saloons.

Breakfast was quickly served in a small crowded restaurant where steam from the kitchen rolled out past a half door. Grits, we had, eggs and fried ham. Biscuits with honey topped the meal. Satisfied, we went outside again, immediately missing the warm comfort of the place. Standing side by side, we stared out at the freight wagons, ladies with umbrellas, cowboys on range ponies, local citizens in surreys, at kids running here and there, dogs at their heels, tongues lolling, merchants sweeping off their porches or shoveling snow from their walkways, and I asked:

'It's a big town, Szabo, where do we start looking?'

'It'll be easier to find the herd than a man,' he replied thoughtfully. 'There must be some sort of local cattleman's association here, someone to tell us who is buying beef right now. There's that,' he said, 'and the stockyard, wherever that might be. We can find it and start reading brands.'

'All right. We should split up, I suppose. Why don't you look for the cattleman's association – I suppose any cowboy can tell you where it is – and I'll wander down to the stockyard. Same thing – any cowhand I run across will know where that is.'

'That sounds like the way to do it,' Szabo said. 'What do you say we meet back here at noon?' He looked across the street at a saloon called the Red Rooster and suggested, 'Or over there.'

'All right,' I agreed. 'The Red Rooster at noon. Let's hope one of us has some news by then. 'I could feel that my face was grimly set. I was sustaining my anger well. Szabo saw it too. He rested his thick hand on my shoulder and said:

'We'll find them, Montana. Don't worry about it.' He added a warning, 'And don't go off doing anything crazy by yourself!'

'No,' I replied. 'If I find out anything I'll save it until we meet and formulate a plan.'

Satisfied with my answer, Szabo hitched up his trousers and ambled away down the boardwalk. I saw him stop a man and ask a question and continue on his way. Knowing that we had entered town from the north, I knew the stockyards and the railroad depot were not that way, so I crossed the muddy street and entered an alley, heading south.

Before I had gone two blocks I could smell it. Another block beneath my muddy boots took me close enough to the stockyards that I could hear confined, weary cattle lowing. Ahead, too, I saw a railroad spur. There was no locomotive in sight, but four or five cattle cars rested on the siding, ready to be loaded with beef for Kansas and beyond. There were a lot of men wandering here and there among the stock pens. Cowboys perched on corral rails and officious looking little men in town suits had pads of paper and pencils in their hands – prosperous looking cattle buyers. The pens of course were not as crowded with cattle as they would have been if it were spring or summer, but there were enough of them milling in tightly-packed confusion to raise a stink and a ruckus.

I sauntered past the pens, looking for the Diamond brand. No one seemed to be paying much attention to me. After half an hour or so I heard a huffing of steam and a clanking roar and glanced toward the rail spur to see a diamond-stack locomotive backing its way slowly toward the waiting cattle cars. There was some activity near these as well now. I saw three men busy lowering a loading ramp from one of the cars.

I hurried on. Looking across a crowded pen I saw, or thought I saw, a man resembling Bellows wearing a tan town suit, in discussion with a pudgy little man wearing a bowler hat. I started hurriedly towards them.

I could hear gates being opened and a ramp being lowered from another cattle car. The lazing cowboys had slipped down from their perches to begin chousing the steers on board. The trainmen were shouting at each other above the bellow of the locomotive, the startled complaints of the cattle and the whistles and yells of the working cowboys.

I reached the spot where I thought I had seen Grant Bellows, but he had eluded me. Anxiously I circled the pens, shouldering through a group of men who stood watching the balky steers being pushed up the loading ramps. Maybe, I was thinking, I could find the railroad engineer and somehow talk him into holding up the train. It seemed a faint chance, but something had to be done. I passed two men who had their backs to me. With my eyes on the locomotive, the loading platform and the stream of bunched cattle, I did not see their faces.

But as I passed, a hand shot out suddenly, grabbed my shoulder and turned me. A club or length of wood fell against my skull above my right ear and I collapsed to the cattle-churned ground, falling into a dark, swirling void.

Something nudged my shoulder. I pushed it away, but another something shoved at me. I tried to open my eyes, but it took more effort than I seemed able to muster. A raging dizziness filled my skull. The aching behind my eyes was tremendous. I felt my hand pinched as if in a giant vise and I came alert in an instinct of survival. I was surrounded by cattle.

The floor rumbled and swayed underfoot as I leaned against the wall behind me. Through the latticed walls of the cattle car I could see the countryside racing by: farms, snowfields, a small settlement. I shook my head to try to clear it, but that caused more confusing pain to erupt inside my skull. I breathed in the fetid air and it was enough to make me feel like vomiting.

I was locked inside a railroad car with about fifty unhappy milling cattle, their horns fixed like sabers to their skulls, their hoofs potential trampling devices. It was a wonder I hadn't been stomped in my sleep. I looked at my hand where a steer had indeed stepped on me and shook it. It was swollen, purpling, but not broken. I could be grateful for that.

It was all I had to be grateful for. Pressing myself tightly against the wall to avoid accidental goring, I eased toward the door of the cattle car while dumb eyes looked at me, horned heads shook in irritation and hoofs, losing their purchase on the wooden, swaying floor of the car, stamped angrily. I made my unsteady way across the floor which, naturally, was slick underfoot. Any mis-step could have dire consequences. If I hit the floor among them, startling the normally docile animals, I might not rise again from beneath panicked hoofs.

My fingers reached out and found a bar fixed to the door. If I could grip it enough to fractionally open the door and slip out through the opening, I would have to risk a leap from the freight train which was now gaining speed and soon would be rushing across the long plains at a speed that would make jumping suicidal.

I tried the door, tugged with all of my strength until my shoulder seemed ready to pop out of its socket. It was no use. The door was obviously locked to deter thieves. I was going to have to ride the freight to the end of the line.

Wherever that might be.

As the train rumbled on, my legs trembled yet I could not risk sitting. The air was close. I did not know how many hours, how many miles more I would be able to remain on my feet. The land rolled past; the cattle milled unhappily, and I continued to roll on, far away from any chance I had had at saving what should have been Tag's and Amy's inheritance.

It seemed that I was just about useless as an avenging angel. I had lost the trail of Jason Grier and his gang, leaving the punishment due them for murdering Sad Sam undelivered. Then I had been given a second chance at salvation – the chance to save Diamond for the kids, and I had failed again.

I thought that I should have stayed where I belonged, alone and isolated in the high mountains where no one needed me, where I could not fail in someone's expectations, where all that was required of me was that I rise, work the long day checking my traps, a long night's sleep and a repetition of the cycle. I knew that expecting much more of Brian McCulloch was to put your faith in a man who was bound to disappoint.

The cattle train lurched and clanked and rambled on through the long day and into the longer night.

EIGHT

You always hear people talk about a man being asleep on his feet, but I had never believed it could be taken literally until the sudden jerk of the cattle car brought my eyes open and I found myself still standing against its door with bright new daylight gleaming through the lattice work of the walls. I had slept the night away, and as sick and battered as I was, I had not fallen beneath the cattle hoofs.

It was a nightmarish way to waken, standing among these wide-eyed, frightened, smelly beasts, their overheated bodies pressing against me. None of them, as it happened, were Diamond steers – I had had time enough to stare at the brands on their flanks. The cattle car jerked again and I peered out to see that we were stopping at some small settlement. The name of the place was painted on a water tank, but I could not read it through the latticed siding. Once more the car jerked and I heard the squeal of brakes, saw that we were slowing and saw a man walking along a platform not thirty feet from where I stood. I began desperately pounding on the side of the car. The man in overalls, wearing a dirty flop hat turned his head my way, but walked on.

I began to shout at the top of my lungs. I saw released steam flow along the platform, heard two men shouting at each other and looked in vain for the man in overalls.

He passed by again, apparently returning from whatever business he had had at the front of the train. I pounded on the wall, shouting at the top of my lungs. Again the man glanced my way; again he continued on, shuffling out of my view. I felt myself beginning to collapse in defeat. I could not survive another day in this living hell. Could not! I leaned my head against the wall of the cattle car and unashamedly wept.

Again I pounded against the wall, my blows growing more feeble, and I heard, felt the locomotive building up a fresh head of steam. We were ready to travel on after taking on a new load of fuel and water for the boiler. The train lurched and I cursed the cattle behind me. The train rolled forward – only a few feet, it seemed – and I heard some shouting outside. Someone laughed which seemed to me like unnecessary torment.

I heard bootsteps. Peering through the lattice I saw the man in overalls returning. This time he carried a ring of heavy keys and a pry bar and my heart leaped with excitement. I began pounding, yelling, screaming. A laconic voice called back.

'I heard you. No sense tiring yourself out, friend.'

There was a sequence of sounds I could almost visualize. Searching for the right key, fitting it, the unsnapping of the hasp, the swinging back of the bar on rusty hinges. Then the door slid open, barely inches, letting in a band of yellow light. Then enough of a gap appeared for me to slip through.

'Get out of there fast,' the same voice advised. 'Them cattle think they're getting out and they'll trample you down trying to get to the door.'

I slid out rapidly, bruising my arm and shoulder. Hitting the platform I was surprised to find that I could barely stand up again under my own power. The man in overalls slammed the cattle car door shut again, locked it and turned frowning eyes on me.

'Just what in hell were you doing in there, cowboy? Did you miss your steers that much?'

'No. It's a long story, mister. I'm just glad you heard me yelling.'

'I didn't hear you yelling. Can't hear much above the noise those critters make. But I did hear you knocking, and much as those steers want to get out of the cattle cars, they seldom knock to have the door opened.'

The train chuffed steam again, and I saw someone wave from the cab of the locomotive. The train drew out of the station, slowly gaining speed and in minutes it was gone, vanishing over the long horizon. The land here was all the yellow of dry grass, nearly featureless, though I could see some far distant mountains. I looked at the station, standing alone on the prairie and asked:

'What's the name of this place?'

'Barlow Tanks,' the man in the overalls told me.

'Where is the town?' I asked.

'Town? There isn't a town around here, stranger.

This is just a railroad watering stop. I don't believe there's what you'd call an actual town for near a hundred miles.'

'Then . . . where am I?'

'Right here.' He squinted at me. 'Where did you come from?'

'Laramie.' I had walked to the unpainted siding of the depot. I leaned against it for support.

'Laramie, Wyoming?' The man shook his head. 'That's quite a way, friend. You're in Nebraska now.'

'Nebraska? I couldn't be!'

'You could be and you are. What'd you say your name was?' I hadn't but I told him just to call me Montana. 'How long were you aboard that train, Montana?'

'I don't know,' I had to admit.

'Running wide open that locomotive can move at forty miles an hour, friend,' he told me. 'That's quite a long way overnight.'

'Yes,' I said in a stunned voice. 'I guess it is. Tell me, how can I get back to Laramie?'

'Buy a ticket on the next train heading that way.'

'I haven't any money,' I told him.

'Well, then I don't know,' he said. 'No money for the train, none for a horse – we haven't any anyway. I'd guess you're stuck in Barlow Tanks for a while, unless you are up to walking back, and I don't think you are.'

'No,' I agreed, 'I'm not.'

He had pulled a large steel watch from his pocket. Glancing at it, he told me, 'I've work to do, young man. My name's Lem Pitt. If I think of any way that I might be able to help, I'll let you know. I hate to see a man completely stranded.'

Completely stranded was what I was, I thought as I watched Lem amble away toward the freight office. No money. No horse. As the man said I was in no shape to walk back to Laramie – which if Lem was right was four or five hundred miles away! I looked down the parallel silver railroad tracks to the east, then to the west. They ran away to infinity and I was stuck in the center of an empty universe.

I found a well around back, drank from the oaken bucket and poured some of the water over my head. The wind was dry, cool, the sky unblotted by clouds. What now? I was hungry, weary, lost. I thought miserably of Laurel and the kids, hopefully waiting for my return bringing them good news about the money from the cattle sale. Instead, I reflected, Grant Bellows and Cole would have ridden on, their purses stuffed. Unless Szabo had had some luck. I thought of that for a moment, letting that small hope buoy my spirits a little, though Szabo, as strong and committed as he was, had been little likely to accomplish much to solve things. It did not matter. I would probably never see Diamond again.

There was a long porch in the back of the windowless station where an overhang provided some shade. I perched on it, resting my weary bones. I stared blankly out at the long plains, not an idea of how to solve my predicament coming to me. I thought of trying to hop a train west when one came through, but it seemed unlikely I could even succeed at that. I thought of begging some kind engineer for a ride, but I would be refused. If they took pity on every vagrant, the railroad would make no profit from ticket sales. I sagged back, resting on my elbows.

Around the corner strode a lanky, cheerful-appearing blond kid. I say 'kid', but he was at least my age, probably a few years older. In his hand he was carrying a wrapped bundle which even my inexperienced eye recognized for the whiskey bottle that it was. Seeing me, he paused briefly and then came ahead, hopping up onto the porch beside me.

'I didn't know anyone was around,' he said affably. 'I'm Drew Tango. Ever heard of me?' he asked with vague hope.

'No, sorry. I'm Brian McCulloch. Some call me Montana.' As I introduced myself he had been unwrapping the whisky bottle. Now he popped the cork with his teeth and offered it to me. I shook my head. There was no telling what that firewater would do to my empty stomach. He shrugged and tipped the bottle up, drinking, deeply.

'I guess you're pretty well known around here,' I tried. That seemed to please him. He cuffed his lips dry.

'You could say so. Not only here, but all up and down the line. I've had my day in the sun, as they say, though I hate to boast.'

It seemed he did not mind boasting, but that was all right with me. His company was a diversion from my deeper concerns.

'What is it you do exactly?' I asked. He looked at me with astonishment, and I added hastily, 'As I say, I'm from Montana and don't know much.'

'Montana,' he told me, adopting that nickname as everyone else readily did, 'I am a railroad detective. The youngest and the best they have.'

'Must be interesting,' I said, reflecting that any idea I had had about hopping a freight without paying had just been crushed.

'It has been, I could tell you . . .' He told me nothing while he took another long drink of the amber liquid in the bottle. He nodded at the Colt revolver that still rode on my hip. 'I suppose you think that you're good with that pistol,' he said cheerfully but challengingly.

'No,' I replied honestly. 'I'm not. I never learned how to shoot well.'

'What? That's nearly a crime out here, Montana. I could show you – I will show you something, but not here. Clements – he's station-master – and old Lem don't like me shooting around the station. Let's take a little walk.'

'All right,' I agreed, having nothing else to do except sit around feeling sorry for myself.

Drew Tango and I walked away from the station across the half-dry land where only sumac and sage seemed to grow, Tango still carrying his whiskey bottle. At a dry creekbed where a desolate, broken willow tree stood, he uncorked his bottle, took another long drink, placed the bottle on the ground, and nodded.

'All right, Montana,' he said in a slightly slurred voice. 'I'll show you. Pick up a couple of those dirt clods.'

'All right,' I answered, bending to the task.

'Not those,' he said, stopping me. 'Too big. Two about that size,' he instructed, toeing a walnut-sized clod. Finding one that matched it in size I showed them to Tango. He nodded. Drew Tango appeared as if he were almost ready to fall asleep on his feet. His eyelids were only slits. Nevertheless he nodded to me and said, 'Throw them as high as you can, Montana.'

I looked at him again to make sure I understood his meaning. At his nod I flung the two rocks as high as I possibly could and watched their flight. Before they could begin their fall back to earth there were two explosions near me and as I watched both clods disappeared in clouds of dust. Before I could look back, Tango had holstered his pistol again. Leaning to pick up the bottle, he drank from it.

Around the cork in his mouth he told me, 'Of course you'll never get as good as I am, Montana, but I can give you some help with your shooting.'

I stared in awe at the railroad detective. I had never seen fancy shooting before, certainly nothing like that with a handgun. Now, I could pick off a squirrel with my rifle, but this was something else. Tango shot without apparent deliberation, purely by instinct. I asked him about it.

'What good are sights on a pistol, really?' he asked with a disparaging smile. 'No good for a close fight, that's for sure. If the man you want is standing that far off, why, grab your Winchester. A gunfight is going to be at close range, and speed is a lot more important than your skill at aiming. Listen, Montana – when you pick up a rock and chuck it at something, do you stand deliberating and aiming? Of course not. A handgun is for blasting away up close. It's speed that's the trick.'

'But speed can't be developed – can it'?' I asked Tango who was now definitely swaying on his feet. He backed up a few steps to lean against the gray trunk of the broken willow tree.

' 'Course it can. The main thing is to practice. Just practice getting that Colt out of your holster and cocked before the other man can. I'll show you a few ways to make the move smoother.'

I waited a while before Tango, now obviously on the edge of drunkenness, drank again and asked challengingly:

'Have you ever had to gun a man down, Montana?'

'No. No, I haven't.'

'Don't let thinking about it get in your way!' he ordered me with alcohol-induced truculence. 'Draw and fire, that's all! Don't think of another thing. For example,' he said, leaning forward, bent at the waist now, raising his eyes to me, 'don't ever think of trying to just wing a man. That makes no sense. Aim at his full body and you've a good chance of tagging him. On the other hand . . . trying to pick a target, aiming for an arm or a leg, the chances are you'll just miss altogether.

'Besides,' he muttered in a barely audible voice, 'men die from leg and arm wounds, don't they?'

I had had enough instruction for the day, I figured, and suggested that we walk back to the railroad station, but Tango wouldn't let me go. His eyes flashed and he gave me a harsh order.

'The time to practice is now!' he roared. 'The time

to practice is every minute you can. Let me see you draw and fire fifty times. You stop when I tell you to because I've seen something you're doing wrong. I'll teach you to draw that Colt until it jumps out of its holster like a rattlesnake striking.'

'Sure, some day when we have the time and I've plenty of ammunition.'

'You've got the time now,' Tango bellowed. 'Where else are you going, what else have you got to do today? As for the ammunition, I've got plenty.'

I felt like declining the rough invitation, but I was the one who had asked for a lesson and besides, Tango was not in the mood to be refused.

I shot. I drew and fired until my right thumb was blistered. Tango badgered me, criticizing the way my elbow was positioned, the squint in my eyes as I pulled the trigger, the involuntary flinch I made when the report of the big .44 revolver sounded.

'Don't sit there admiring your draw!' he shouted after I had made what I thought was a good shot. 'Pump a second bullet through that revolver's barrel. How do you know the first round was enough to do the job!'

It went on like that for what seemed like hours. Each time I thought that Tango was so drunk that he must have fallen asleep or passed out, I would hear him bark at me, criticizing the angle of my wrist, or the way I braced my feet. The sun rode higher and then began to coast over toward the western mountains. I had a pile of brass cartridge casings at my feet and my nostrils felt scorched by the amount of gunpowder I had spent. I looked again to Tango, begging for a rest.

Except that by this time he was truly passed out. Propped against the tree still, bottle in his hand, he was unmoving, unseeing. I walked to him, crouched and picked him up in a fireman's carry, lugging him back toward the railroad station.

I placed him gently on the porch, sitting him against the wall. His hand had not fallen from the neck of the whiskey bottle. I stepped away, perspiration staining my shirt, and stared at Drew Tango in amazement. He was a different sort of man than any I had encountered before in my brief life. I shook my head and walked around toward the front platform of the station. I met Lem Pitt almost immediately.

'Are you still hanging around here?' he asked gruffly.

'I've got no place to go,' I answered and he smiled, scratching his whiskered chin.

'A man could starve to death around here, Montana. Clement, the station master, he wouldn't let me feed a stray dog. That would be wasteful. Everything we have here is goods delivered by the railroad, and sometimes they forget to ship our orders. Then I have to go out hunting for quail, cottontails and such. I don't care what they say, a man can't live on birds and rabbit meat alone.' His cloudy eyes brightened slightly and he looked across my shoulder.

'Say, where is that so-called railroad detective of ours?'

He already knew the answer, but I told him anyway. Apparently drinking was a constant problem with Drew Tango. Lem said, 'I wonder where he keeps that liquor stashed,' and went away shaking his head.

I sat down on the edge of the platform, returning my thoughts to the problems I had, rubbing the raw skin of my right hand. Lem had returned and there was some anxiety on his face.

'Clement is raising hell. The six o'clock train is due in any minute. There's some men on board – mine bosses from Colorado – carrying gold with them. They paid good money to pick up a guard here at Barlow to help watch for trouble before they reach the more settled lands where there have been all those train robberies. Where'd you say Tango was sleeping it off?'

I told him, and got to my feet as Lem rushed around the corner of the depot. I stood watching up the line for the train, revisiting my notion of trying to catch a free ride on it, though the plan had little chance of success, especially if the men riding it were carrying a lot of money and bound to be wary of strangers. Especially those who looked like me.

I knew I still stank of the long ride droving with the herd, of a grueling cross-country walk, of traveling in a cattle car, but I had caught a glimpse of myself in a window pane and was startled by what I saw. Unshaven, the fresh scar on my cheek distinct and raw-looking, my clothes rumpled and stained, I looked like a roughneck hobo. I thought with fond remembrance of the last hot bath I had taken in the Diamond ranch house . . . and briefly of the dark-eyed woman who had been there at the time.

Lem returned.

'Darned fool!' he said, looking back. 'He knew he was supposed to catch this train.'

'You couldn't wake Tango?'

'I couldn't have roused him with a bugle! Don't know why he acts like that.' Lem removed his blue railroad cap and scratched at his sparse white hair. 'I guess it has something to do with some of the things he's had to do – killing men. That's no way to make a living if you ask me.

'Now what are we supposed to do!' he asked, growing mournful. 'The station master will jump down my throat as well, as if it's my fault that Drew Tango got himself tanked again.' Lem's eyes brightened, but the sudden intelligence I saw there was of the cunning sort. He smiled lopsidedly and put a friendly hand on my shoulder. I was wary of the gesture. I had an idea what he was going to say.

'You want out of here, don't you, Montana?'

'If there's a way.'

'There is, and it's simple. It will get us all off the hook – you, me, Clement and Drew Tango.' I expressed my question with my eyes. Lem Pitt patted my shoulder again.

'You just take Tango's place guarding these mine bosses and their gold. A free train ride out of here and no one the wiser, no one hurt.'

'I don't think I can—'

Lem interrupted me. 'Look, I know you're no Drew Tango with a gun but the odds of being held up are slim to none. Once that locomotive gets up to speed, it's as safe as picking daisies. Otherwise Tango loses his job, the railroad comes down hard on me and Clement for not watching him, and you – you get to wander the prairies until you starve to death.'

That didn't leave me an option that I could see. As Lem finished speaking, the distant sound of a locomotive whistle lifted my head. I could see the plume of white smoke on the horizon. My heart skipped a little.

'Is that it?' I asked Lem.

'Yes, sir.' He glanced at his watch. 'Right on time, too.'

'Lem . . . that's an eastbound train.'

It would take me far away from Laramie, far away from Diamond and a million miles from my Montana home.

NINE

I didn't like the way that Drew Tango's gold railroad detective badge rode on my shirt front. Apparently the gentlemen in their business suits sharing the Pullman car I rode on thought it fit me poorly as well. None of them said as much directly to me, but I knew the shape I was in, the way my raggedy clothes and unshaven face appeared, and I caught occasional disapproving glances from behind their gold-rimmed spectacles. They had paid the railroad good money to have their money guarded by me!

Drunk and disheveled, Drew Tango would have put in a better appearance than I did, exuding confidence as he did. I was incompetent as a gunhand, and I knew it. I stood in the back of the luxurious railroad car with its velvet curtains and round mahogany tables, trying to be inconspicuous. My eyes, for the most part, I kept on the endless flat scenery rolling by.

When I could no longer take the constant scrutiny and ill-concealed mistrust, I eased out of the car, crossed the space between that platform and the next and entered a much less luxurious car where people sat in rows, men behind newspapers, children bouncing on the cushions of the seats, ladies fanning themselves with lacy fans, bored cattlemen, legs stretched into the aisles, watching the flat miles flow past. None of these looked like hold-up artists.

'They're not much company, are they?' the lady asked, smiling up at me.

'Pardon me?'

'Those stuffed shirts in their private car. Bankers, mine owners, land merchants. Why, only a few years ago most of them were prospectors, drifters, ne'er-do-wells. I've known them all since I was a little girl.'

I took a closer look at the lady who was speaking. I couldn't guess her age, somewhere this side of thirty, her sort of silvery blond hair pinned up in a roll beneath her wide black straw hat. She wore a dark blue dress that nearly matched her eyes. Her mouth was generous and amused at some inner comedy.

'You seem to know them well,' I said, leaning back against the partition for support.

'Why don't you sit down before you fall down,' she said, patting the seat beside her.

'Sorry,' I said sheepishly. 'Things have gone kind of rough for me lately. I didn't know it showed.'

I gratefully sat on the blue cushioned seat beside her and removed my hat, wiping my tangled hair back with my fingers. I grinned. 'I'm sorry about my appearance.'

'No need to apologize,' she answered. 'I've been around hard-working men all my life. Beneath a rough exterior. . . .' she said, not finishing the quote.

'Mine's pretty rough,' I said with a laugh. 'If I could

tell you my story, you'd understand.'

'There's time,' she said, inclining her head toward the plains which rolled past endlessly beyond the window of the train. 'We won't hit Kansas City for a long while.'

'Kansas City! Is that where this train is going?'

She looked at me, smiled quirkily and asked, 'You didn't even know that much – where you are going?'

'Not exactly,' I was forced to admit. 'You see, Miss. . . .'

'Gloria. Miss Gloria Washburn. One of those fat cats in the Pullman is my father, George Washburn, Esquire. Formerly known as Peanuts Washburn.'

I smiled again, this woman had a wry sense of humor that I warmed up to immediately.

'You see, Miss Washburn . . .' She wagged a finger at me and I started again. 'You see *Gloria*, I am riding the rails as a sort of temporary rail detective. I just hope for everyone's sake that there is no trouble on the way to Kansas City. I managed to get myself into a predicament,' I said and went on to tell her most of what had happened to me since leaving Montana. She listened with interest, and I found it made me feel better for the telling. No gunmen or robbers interrupted us. The only event causing my narrative to break off was when a small boy from the front of the car bounced his rubber ball errantly and it flew toward us. Gloria scooped it up easily and tossed it back to the shame-faced kid who was being scolded by his mother.

'And how,' Gloria asked when I had finished, 'are you planning on returning to Wyoming now?'

'That's the question, isn't it? Not being a paid railroad employee, I'll just end up in Kansas City as broke and hungry as ever. I suppose I'll try to find some kind of rough work there, enough to make money for train fare back to Laramie.'

'Listen,' Gloria said. She had leaned forward intently, her small hands clasped together. She stared at the floor of the train for a minute before continuing. 'I'll speak to my father, the illustrious George Washburn, Esquire.'

'Formerly known as "Peanuts",' I said, and she laughed and nodded.

'I'll talk to Dad. He has a lot of contacts. He may be able to find something for you besides loading hay bales or sweeping the streets.'

'You have no idea how much I'd appreciate that,' I said honestly. I liked this woman and believed her when she gave her promise. Yet how long would it take for me to earn even enough for my railroad fare? So much could have happened back on Diamond by now. Had Szabo managed to do anything? Had Grant Bellows even bothered to return to the ranch after the cattle sale? Were Amy and Tag on the brink of being destitute? Was Laurel. . . . I thanked Gloria again and we rode amicably the rest of the way into Kansas City.

The train chuffed, huffed, clanked, whistled and moaned its way into the station at Kansas City. As it finally came to a screeching stop, Gloria reached into the reticule she carried and then touched my hand. She had given me a ten-dollar gold piece and a calling card.

'I can't—'

'You find yourself a respectable place to sleep tonight, a place that offers baths!' she instructed me, wrinkling her nose, 'and order a decent meal. Tomorrow you will come to call on me and Peanuts, and we will see about finding you some work.'

I had thought of Laramie as a big town. Kansas City overwhelmed me with its noise and bustle. As I made my way along the streets I saw nothing but surly, angry faces. Now, I like people, but in smaller bunches. In Kansas City they bumped shoulders with you, glowered and pushed by. I wondered why, if they were all as unhappy living here as they seemed, they didn't up and leave. But maybe that was because I was seeing things through a stranger's eyes, or because I myself had the overpowering urge to get shot of this place and back to the stark, wild lands of the north.

I found a hotel that looked a notch up from a flophouse, a few shelves below what you would call plush accommodation, and signed myself in. The building, yellow brick on the outside, had three stories. I was given a room on the second floor, at the end of an unlighted corridor. I guess the room wasn't much, but I liked the place. I hadn't spent many nights of my life in a real bed. I walked out into the corridor and met a young dark-headed guy with a batch of fresh towels over his arm and asked him about a bath and the possibility of finding a razor. He was accommodating and cheerful and within half an hour they had brought hot water up to the bath on my floor, furnished me with soap and a razor. After eating I was ready to present myself to the world.

Purchasing a clean yellow shirt which I changed into at the store, I started looking for 'Peanuts,' Mr Charles Washburn, Esquire. I didn't plan to go to his house or place of business until morning: the two of them would be as weary from travel as I was, but I wanted to have an idea of where to find him. It seemed that was no problem. Mr Charles Washburn was well known in town, and lived in an affluent section of the city called Northridge.

That settled, I wandered the streets for a time, fighting off the urge for another Kansas City steak dinner and finally, at sundown gave in to my exhaustion and returned to the hotel early.

Morning was bright with sun although there was a haze over the city from the various industrial plants there. It was cold outside, and I wondered how the weather was up on the northern plains. I could do nothing about returning there now, not until I had some money in my pockets, and so I started out walking away from the heart of the city into a sort of isolated pocket of fine homes and massive oak trees.

I found the house easily. There was a wrought iron sign announcing the owner's name out front hanging from a white painted brick pillar. At the doorway of the tall porticoed house I rapped three times, turned my back briefly to study the layout of the city beyond and turned to knock again.

Gloria Washburn opened the door before my knuckles touched wood. Her eyes were bright, her silvery blond hair down around her shoulders. She was only half-awake, half-dressed. She clutched the neck of

115

the blue wrapper she wore together.

'I'm sorry,' I said. 'If it's too early I can come back later.'

'It's all right,' she said with a smile that seemed genuine and she motioned me into the enormous house, stepping aside for me to pass. 'You've cleaned up some,' she said.

'Well, as best I could,' I replied, glancing down at my scuffed boots and faded jeans.

'Father is up already,' Gloria said. 'I'm not sure that he slept at all last night. Something is troubling him. I'll show you where his study is, and then if you'll excuse me, I have to dress. I'll have one of the maids bring coffee.'

One of the maids? Whatever Peanuts did for a living, he obviously did it well.

Gloria led me across the house to a ceiling-high oaken door. Without knocking she opened it to reveal Charles Washburn, Esquire sitting behind a wide, polished desk. He now wore spectacles and was dressed in a silky blue dressing gown with a black velvet collar. He glanced up in surprise and then leaned back in his black leather chair, dropping the stack of papers he had been scrutinizing.

'Dad – this is Brian McCulloch,' Gloria said and then she slipped past me and out of the room, leaving the ornately carved door open. Washburn continued to study me for a moment, then his face seemed to brighten a little.

'Now I remember you – from the train. I must say you looked a little rugged then.'

'I'd been long on the trail, Mr Washburn.'

He nodded as if remembering the wandering days of his youth. 'Sit down,' he said, offering me a chair. I was expecting him to be stiff, formal in speech, but in his own home I suppose he was still 'Peanuts' Washburn, and he was not the stodgy sort by nature.

'Gloria tells me she spent a lot of time talking to you. You have her warmest recommendation, McCulloch.'

'Thank you, sir,' I said, not knowing what I had said to deserve a high recommendation or what task it was that I was recommended for. I sat in the stuffed black leather chair I had been offered, placed my hat on my knee and waited for the man to begin.

'What I want you to do may be hazardous, but not too much so for a man of your background. A railroad detective must find himself in all sorts of little difficulties from time to time.'

I supposed they did, but I was not and never had been a railroad detective. I said nothing; I needed whatever job I could get in the worst way. There were people waiting for me in Wyoming.

'Seriously,' Washburn said, leaning forward in his chair to peer at me through the lenses of his spectacles, 'there should be little danger. It is important that you remain alert for it, however; the job I am offering you is of the utmost importance to me.'

I simply nodded and after a tiny, blue-eyed girl in a white dress and black apron had brought in a silver tray bearing a coffeepot and two sets of cups and saucers and scurried away, Washburn continued.

'I have many interests, Mr McCulloch. Too many, I

sometimes think as I try to juggle them all. I have invested in cattle, in land, in railroads, in the fur trade and mining speculation. This last is what we are now concerned with.' He poured coffee into one of the small white cups and handed it across his desk to me before going on.

'A manufacturer of mining equipment is holding a shipment for me in St Louis. I have either to deliver the funds to him in the next few days or see the equipment auctioned to the highest bidder. My mine in Colorado needs this equipment desperately. I intend to draw a cashier's check from my bank today. . . .'

I continued to listen, yet some part of my mind had been drawn up by his mention of St Louis. Was I to continue traveling east, farther away from Diamond and its troubles, from Tag and Amy? From Laurel. . . ?

'There is little threat of anyone trying to take the check from you,' Washburn was saying. 'No one else but Bill Wanamaker can cash it. But if the check is somehow delayed, lost or pilfered, I will lose my option on the equipment. Do you understand the situation?'

'Perfectly,' I commented. He rose then as if our negotiations were at an end, adding only belatedly:

'A hundred dollars, would you say is acceptable to act as my courier?'

A hundred dollars? Of course it was acceptable. That would get me back to Wyoming, allow me to purchase a decent if not flashy horse and see me comfortably along the way. We shook hands as I became aware of Gloria Washburn's presence in the open doorway behind me.

118

'Everything settled then?' she asked. She had managed to dress and brush and pin up her hair while Peanuts and I spoke.

'We have an understanding,' Washburn said. 'I'm sure that Detective McCulloch will handle matters capably. The railroad, after all, does not hire incompetents.' Thoughtfully he asked, 'Will this interfere with your regular duties, McCulloch?'

'No, sir. I'll just let them know that I'm taking a brief leave of absence.'

'Good! I wouldn't want to make trouble for you. Now then, if you'll give me a few minutes I'll write down Bill Wanamaker's address for you and if you would accompany me to the bank. . . ? Good. I'll draw the cashier's check and see that your wages are provided. I thank you, Mr McCulloch. It's fortunate that my daughter happened to encounter you.'

I suppose it was fortunate. Outside of what was left from the money Gloria had slipped me I was destitute, without work, battered, alone and far from home. Now at least part of my problems had been solved. Though I was still traveling *away*. Away from Wyoming. I waited while Washburn summoned a surrey and went to shave and dress. Gloria and I stood close together, saying little.

'I can't thank you enough,' I began but she silenced me.

'It's nothing. Father needed a chore done and you can do it for him. If I was any help to you, I'm glad.'

'If I ever get back this way, Gloria. . . .'

She smiled at me and shook her head. 'You won't be

119

back,' she said. 'I know that.' She paused and let her blue eyes drift up to meet mine, briefly taking my hands. 'Tell whoever she is that I think she's a lucky woman.'

TEN

It was snowing when the train pulled out of Kansas City. Winter had arrived across the world; it seemed to blanket all of the city's sharp edges, muting colors and motion. I had a cashier's check for ten thousand dollars in a zippered bag riding in my coat pocket, money that was extremely important to Peanuts Washburn, and so I kept a wary eye out as I rode. Seated in the last car, my back against the wall I saw no one who looked like trouble. It was true, as Washburn had said, that no one but the intended recipient could cash the check, but men will steal when they think they see an opportunity only to discover later that they have something that is of no use.

I knew that the figure $10,000 on the face of the check might cause someone's eyes to light up no matter that the money was supposedly non-negotiable by anyone but this Bill Wanamaker, or at least that was what I had been told. I wasn't even sure about that. Thieves had a better understanding of how these things worked than I did. I just knew that I was determined to guard the money. For Washburn.

For Gloria. I liked that woman although there was no romantic spark between us. She seemed honest, cheerful and devoted to her father: strong positive traits.

The train rumbled on across the snowy countryside. Another new storm was in the offing. I could feel it in the air. I lowered my hat, crossed my arms and rode on in peaceful silence.

They didn't make their move until we slowed to pick up water and fuel at a tiny settlement named Corcoran, Kansas. I hadn't noticed them before because they didn't look the part. The short, dumpy man in a blue town suit was with a lanky, red haired man who I had taken for his son or a younger relative. Striding toward the back of the car as the train slowed, they were suddenly beside me, both of them exhibiting handguns. The portly man smiled and spoke softly:

'We'd like to see what you're holding in your coat.'

I have no idea how they knew that I was carrying anything in my coat. I suppose Peanuts and I had unwisely transacted our business on the station platform while others watched. It did not matter how they knew; they knew. I mentally fumbled for an answer. The other passengers had risen as well, peering out the fogged windows, some wanting a chance to get off the train and stretch their legs. I still had not come up with an answer for the men with the guns.

I decided to run for it.

I kicked out at the short man, caught him in the belly and wheeled out of my seat to slam through the door behind me. I knew instantly that I had made a mistake.

They had not wished to risk shooting in the crowded railroad car, but I was in the open now. They could do their killing and come up with a story later. I still didn't appear to be the most reputable of men. The law could be told that I was the robber.

I slipped off the platform of the railroad car, raced forward, felt my boot skid on the steel of a railroad track and went down roughly onto the gravel there. The clumsy move proved to be a boon. A gunshot sounded near at hand and the bullet whipped past my head. Had I been standing, I would have taken it.

Scrambling on hands and knees, I rushed on. By the time I had gotten to my knees they were off the train and I was faced with a six-foot high station platform. I started to climb it, changed my mind and pawed at the Colt revolver under my coat flap.

Four gunshots sounded as rapidly as a woodpecker's tapping and I looked up to see the little man fall to the ground. His accomplice clutched his chest, howled at the sky and tumbled to the earth as well.

I had not fired a shot.

Standing there, panting, my Colt heavy in my hand I just stared at the dead men, at the railroad workers rushing to the site. The voice behind me barked out mockingly:

'I told you not to aim that thing, Montana. Point and fire. Shooting's as easy as throwing rocks. Just do it quick!'

I looked up to see Drew Tango standing on the railroad platform, calmly reloading his smoking pistol.

ELEVEN

The train rumbled on. The excitement over the shooting had died down. The passengers rode silently eastward. I finally asked Drew Tango, who rode beside me:

'How did you happen to show up?'

With a smile, the blond man answered, 'I'm a railroad detective, Montana. You know that.'

'But . . . the railroad didn't fire you?'

'They fire me all the time,' Drew said with a laugh. 'I may not be dependable, but I'm the best man they have and they know it.'

'So you're going through to St Louis?'

'Over and back, over and back again – it's like that, this job of mine. Tedious, really. Then every now and then there's a minute of excitement.' He saw the way I was looking at him and answered my unasked question, 'I'm here because a certain Mr Washburn asked the railroad to make sure that a courier of his had some extra protection.'

'I never saw you,' I said dully. Tango laughed and slapped my shoulder.

'You're not supposed to see me, Montana! What good's a detective that everyone notices?'

I smiled and shrugged. I had to admit that Tango was good at his job. I couldn't judge if he was the best man riding the rails, but he had sure pulled my bacon from the fire this time.

'You need a few more shooting lessons,' he commented as the train picked up speed. 'Man, did you look clumsy out there.'

Tango was a good traveling companion, and he unreeled a lot of interesting and amusing stories on our ride. The one thing I noticed he did not mention was any shooting skirmishes he must have had over the years he had been riding the rails. Apparently it made him uncomfortable to speak of his fights, and so I did not inquire too deeply. It could be that he was the unhappiest sort of man – a hired killer who did not like to kill.

I had thought Kansas City large until we hit St Louis. There was a bustle, a sort of controlled anxiety about the mobs of people swarming the streets, the plants, the waterfront. I took my first look at the Mississippi River and had the same thought – I thought I had seen wide-running rivers before, but here was one you could not even see across. All in all, it made me realize what I truly was – a rural boy roaming the big city.

And I did not like it. Some people, I know, like the excitement of such places. I only wanted to leave the city, all cities far behind and return to the Plains. I don't know how often I thought of the Diamond and the trouble the kids might be in, but such thoughts hurried me along my way as I looked for Bill Wanamaker. I don't know how many times I thought of Laurel and her warm smile either, but it was often.

Tango guided me to a small hotel he had stayed at in the past. Registering there I noticed that there was a saloon downstairs. Drew said, 'I'll be around waiting for you when you've finished your business.'

I eyed him doubtfully, but the blond detective smiled and put both hands on my shoulders, saying, 'Don't worry about me, Montana. I have in mind drinking a couple of beers and trying my hand at a game of faro. Truth be told, I am starting to lose my desire for that hard liquor life.'

I took him at his word, besides, what difference was it to me if he wanted to drink his life away? He was someone I'd met in passing, and I happened to like Drew Tango, but we would likely never see one another again, and anyway I did not pretend to understand what had gone on in his life, nor was I so sure of the rightness of my own life to wish to change his ways.

I wandered the waterfront for a little while, amazed by the size and majesty of the big paddle-wheeling steamboats passing out on the big muddy river, by the shouted confusion surrounding the hundred of flatboats docking, loading, unloading; the sprawl of life on the docks was far beyond my experience. I passed the sign almost without noticing it. Then I paused and turned, read it again and stood immobilized, hands on my hips. My mouth may have been hanging open a little. Must have been – a pair of river sailors passed and one of them called out, 'Hey rube!'

I stood still gawking at the professionally lettered sign fastened to the side of a red-brick two-story building. It read:

'Jason Grier & Associates. Fur Traders.'

I started towards it, halted in the middle of the cobblestone street as buggies and men on horseback passed, and turned reluctantly back. First things first, I told myself. I had to find Bill Wanamaker and complete my assignment. I had, after all, promised Peanuts and Gloria, and I had been paid for the job. There would be time later to do what must be done. I had found Jason Grier, or rather chance events had taken me to the doorstep of the killer who had shot down Sad Sam in that Montana forest. The heat of my anger traveled with me as I went into the heart of the business district toward Wanamaker's manufacturing concern.

Wanamaker proved to be a wiry, balding man with one eye that refused to focus. As soon as I was shown into his office and revealed the purpose behind my visit, he began smiling, pacing the room with delight.

'I can't tell you what a relief this is, McCulloch. I rushed the equipment through production but since then I've just been sitting on it, waiting for Washburn to send me this payment so we could ship it. This is fine, just fine!' He shook my hand three or four times before ushering me out of his office.

At least someone was going to have a good day.

I unbuttoned my coat, checked the feel of my Colt in its holster and started back uptown toward Jason Grier's place of business. I wished distantly that I had Drew Tango at my side, but this was none of his affair. I would have to learn to take care of business myself. Sad Sam was no longer with me to make all of the important decisions.

When I again reached the door of the fur trading building, I found it locked. An almost indecipherable sign pinned there informed me that they had closed early. And added, 'Business to be conducted at rear.'

I went to the rear, meaning to conduct some business.

What I found was an open bay where hundreds of pelts were being stacked and graded, waiting to be shipped east or to Europe. Four or five men were there, working busily, but not pushing themselves since the boss seemed to be away. I stopped a stooped, hook-nosed man carrying a bale of ermine hides on his shoulder.

'Where's Grier?' I demanded. He looked at me as if I were of no importance.

'It is the third Thursday of the month – *Mr* Grier always dines at the Antietam Club on third Thursdays.' He smiled, if you could call it that, but the expression only confirmed that he had taken an instant dislike to me. 'Can I give Mr Grier a message?'

'No,' I smiled in a manner that I hoped matched his in unpleasantness. 'I'll have to deliver the message personally.'

The man was still scowling when I left, and by now a few other loyal employees had gathered around. I stepped out into the cool sunshine and started on my way. Then I spied a small pen just across the alley. The sorrel horse there lifted its head, nickered and circled the yard once. It knew me. I knew him. It was Santana, the horse Grier had taken from me in Montana.

Happy and angry at once I walked to the yard as the sorrel continued to watch me expectantly. Some horses are able to remember their masters as well as a dog can. Santana was one such animal. There was a wire loop holding the gate and I slipped it off and entered the yard.

'What are you doing!' I heard a voice behind me call out as I stroked Santana's nose and took his bridle in hand. Glancing back I saw three men from the shop rushing toward me. I turned, unbuttoned my coat once again and waited.

'What are you doing? That's Mr Grier's horse!' the man with the hooked nose yelled. He was bent over nearly double, fists clenched with excitement. I loosened my Colt in its holster just enough for them to consider matters.

'The hell it is,' I said and I led Santana out of there, brushing past the angry knot of men.

I told Drew Tango what had happened that day.

'So what now?' he asked. We were seated at a round table in the saloon adjacent to our hotel. If Drew had been thinking a lot, it didn't show. He seemed sober and reflective as he waited intently for my answer.

'Find this club, the Antietam, confront Jason Grier and. . . .'

'Is that the best way to go about things, to proceed with your life?' Tango asked. His eyes were remote, almost gentle. 'I know all about killing, Montana. It won't bring you any satisfaction in the long run. Not as much as you think it will.

'From what you tell me,' he continued, 'you've got a woman and two kids counting on you back in Wyoming. People who trust you and are relying on you. Tell me, Montana, which way do you think Sad Sam would rather have you honor his memory: by getting into a gunfight, with the possibility of you dying as well, or taking care of those people who are counting on you back in Wyoming?'

I made no answer. I knew that Drew Tango was right, but the urge for revenge is a strong emotion, so strong that the wisdom of such a course of action can be lost in its shadows.

'I'll have to think about it,' I said finally. Drew pushed back from the table and rose to his feet, stretching.

'There's a westbound train leaving at nine in the morning, Montana. I'll be on it. I hope you will be too.'

Well, I was. I had Santana loaded in a stock car and my ticket in my hand when I found Tango seated in the first row of the front car. He looked up, smiled, yawned and nodded, but said nothing more about my decision.

That is until we pulled into that same little watering stop, Corcoran, Kansas. We had stepped onto the platform to stretch. Tango had his arms raised over his head, and he was grinning, but his voice was deliberate.

'There's some men watching you, Montana,' he said.

I had seen nothing, but a part of Drew Tangos' job, after all, was to be aware of everything going on around him. Now at his almost imperceptible nod I looked along the length of the train to see three burly men clustered together. They turned their eyes quickly from me. My chest tightened briefly, I wanted to yell, to strike out, but I managed to get myself under control. I told Tango:

'The one with the black beard is Jason Grier.'

'I figured as much,' he replied.

'But why. . . ? How?'

'You announced yourself by taking Santana, didn't you? What else is Grier to do but eliminate you? He can't have you popping up to destroy his reputation as a respectable business man. As to why out here,' Drew waved an arm around, taking in the empty flat expanse of the Kansas prairie, 'this is a much better place to take care of the sort of business he has in mind than in the heart of St Louis.'

He was right, of course. I had little experience in deducing the motives of men. Drew Tango did that for a living. I was suddenly chilled by the thought of what lay before me. Grier wanted me dead. And I knew full well that the man was capable of killing. I was comforted by the thought that I had the seemingly nerveless Drew Tango for a companion.

'What should we do?' I asked.

'Ride it out,' Tango said with seeming indifference. 'They hoped to surprise you. Now they've lost that edge. Just be ready for them when they decide to make their move. Keep your holster slick and remember that Colt is as fast as a snake – as fast as you want it to be. *Just don't think too much.* When it comes time to act, just do it. Try to remember what I taught you – as much as you can,' he said with a little chuckle. Obviously Drew Tango still did not think much of my shooting.

'Drew,' I asked as we re-boarded the train, 'are you standing with me in this?'

'Why, of course, Montana! We're friends . . . besides, I don't allow any mischief on this railroad line.'

We rode in silence as the Chief, as it was called, rolled on across Kansas and toward that small corner of Nebraska we had to pass through. For some reason I didn't understand and didn't care about, we rolled straight past Barlow Tanks. I thought I saw Lem Pitt standing on the platform, but at thirty miles an hour, he was only a blur and I couldn't be sure.

The miles rolled past uneventfully. I never really slept. At any unexpected creak or bang my eyes went to the door of the compartment, expecting to see Grier and his hoodlums rushing at me. The day faded and darkness settled. When I had finally fallen into a half-sleep, I felt Drew nudge me with his elbow. I jerked awake, stared at the night-blackened windows of the railroad car and waited for an explanation.

'Just thought you'd want to know,' Drew Tango said with a grin. 'We're into Wyoming.'

'Can't be!'

'We are. I saw the green railroad sign. You're just not much used to traveling faster than your pony can walk,' Drew said, tilting his hat down over his eyes. He folded his arms and drifted off to sleep himself.

I stared out the windows, unable to believe that the miles had flown by so quickly. A day and a night and a man could be transported from St Louis to Wyoming!

132

The modern times were far beyond my reckoning.

Beyond the window I could see snow drifts and knew that the north country weather had caught up with me again – or I had caught up with it. We were rolling into November now and the world beyond the railroad's glass windows was falling into the days of brittle frost and long hard storms. The blizzard time was upon the north plains: the hard days were coming. . . .

And somewhere, not so many hours ahead, Tag and Amy . . . and Laurel waited. Who knew what condition Grant Bellows' thievery had left them in.

Now sleep, even the thought of it became impossible. As the train rattled on, my blood pulsed, my nerves became jagged. If what I thought was true, Laramie would be the next stop on the line. I had not for a moment forgotten Jason Grier and his crew who were presumably riding with us in another compartment, but they seemed somehow insignificant. I would gladly let them go if they did not hinder my return to Diamond.

I had lost my thirst for vengeance.

When we stepped from the train on that day, the second of November, I had forty-seven dollars in my pocket, a voucher to retrieve Santana from the stock car, a friend at my side and an emotion I could not truly define riding heavy in my heart. It was not anger, not entirely sadness; it was sort of a weariness of the soul that was so deeply troubling it could not be brightened, ignored or dismissed.

'Are they still with us?' I asked Drew Tango, because

133

I knew he had a practiced eye.

'Oh, yes. I saw them crossing between cars on the other side of the tracks,' Drew told me, and he managed a grin.

'I've got to get my horse,' I told him.

'I suppose I'll have to find one to buy,' Tango said, 'if I'm going to ride with you.'

He said it carelessly as if it were a casual thought, but I knew that it was a deeply meant offer to aid a friend. I did not show my gratitude because he would not have wanted me to, but silently I thanked him from the bottom of my heart for his offer.

We walked toward the freight cars where my horse and those of other men were being unloaded along with crates and barrels intended for the merchants of Laramie. We had come within a hundred feet of the holding pen when Tango whispered:

'They're waiting, Montana. It's here that they mean to do it.'

TWELVE

Approaching the horse pen I saw the three of them clearly, although they had tried to assume a stance of nonchalance. Jason Grier was there, leaning against a post to our right. The other two were staked out one on our left, one straight ahead of me across the corral where four young colts and Santana watched our approach with interest. I thought Grier's two sidekicks were the two men I had seen with him when Sad Sam was murdered, but was not sure. My attention had not been on the henchmen that day. Tango sighed audibly.

'I'll take the one to my right,' he told me, nodding toward Jason Grier. 'Try to get the one to your left first. Drop to your knee, you'll have a better chance that way.'

'Drew,' I said, 'this isn't your fight, you know.'

'They're on railroad property, Montana. If they commit a crime here, it's my responsibility.'

I nodded, knowing that he was only pretending that he was not doing this out of friendship – risking his life for me! Why, I was not sure. I walked into the pen as if gathering up Santana was my only aim. Grier could not be fooled; he knew the game and he grabbed for his holstered revolver before I had taken six strides.

That was his last mistake. I saw Drew Tango's hand move – or thought I did – it happened in a flash, heard the roar of his .44 and saw Jason Grier stagger back, his hand still glued to the handle of his holstered Colt.

The horses reared and danced away. Across from me through the milling herd, I saw the burly man with the red beard draw, and I drew as well. I simply drew and shot without aiming, as if I were throwing a stone at him. He swayed on his feet and then pitched forward on his face, quite dead.

I saw the man straight ahead of me bring up his gun, remembered belatedly to go to my knee as Drew had told me, but there was no need for it. The pistol shot from behind me battered my eardrums and I saw the third man buckle.

Drew Tango had shot him as well, and he was surely dead. The horses slowed their panicked milling. I stood, trying to take in a breath. My legs wobbled beneath me. I saw Drew Tango striding toward me. He holstered his pistol with a kind of fancy twirl, but I noticed that his legs were shaking too.

'Hell of a way to make a living,' Tango said, spitting somewhere near the toe of his boot. A crowd had gathered, but they approached cautiously, not wanting to get in the way of any flying lead. 'Let's get out of here,' Tango said, and his suggestion seemed a wise one.

I stood for a moment looking down at Jason Grier, and I wondered – as Tango had asked – if it was all worth it. Not only for me, for Sad Sam, but for Grier as well. It was all a hell of a waste, I decided.

By the time I had thrown a saddle over Santana and slipped him his bit Tango had returned with a sprightly young palomino. He wore a grin as he approached riding the leggy three-year-old.

'Nice looking pony, isn't he?' was all he said, though he was obviously delighted with the frisky animal. 'What do you say we get you home now, Montana?'

'I'm ready,' was my answer, but I was much more than ready. I was eager, needful and determined. The people on the ranch needed me, and perhaps – I thought with sorrow – might believe that I had deserted them in their time of need.

Tango grinned kind of weakly and said to me, 'If it's any consolation, you did better with that pistol this time.'

We started our ponies northward, and the citizens of Laramie let us pass through their ranks without questioning us. I knew then that we were back in the West.

I saw Szabo in the middle of Main Street about the time it began to snow.

The big man stood there, arms stretched skyward in astonishment as he recognized me.

'Lord, Montana, where have you been!'

'Away. And you, Szabo?'

'I'm just broke and stranded,' he said, looking from me to Tango questioningly. I introduced the two. Drew leaned down from his saddle to shake the big man's hand.

137

'Is anybody but me hungry?' Tango asked. 'I haven't had a bite since Kansas City.'

We all agreed that that was a good suggestion. Looking at Szabo, I thought that he might not have eaten in a few days. I was hungry as well, but my thoughts had pushed that consideration aside. Szabo knew of a small nearby eatery and we sat together there catching up on what had happened over the past few days.

'Grant Bellows,' Szabo told us around a mouthful of over-easy eggs and toast with strawberry jam, 'he came up with a deed to Diamond.'

'You can't mean it!'

'I do. And with you gone, me gone and Curly dead . . . who's going to stand for the kids and their rights?'

'Curly,' Drew Tango said tersely, spinning his coffee cup on the red-checked tablecloth. 'Montana told me – you don't mean Curly Sledge by any chance.'

Szabo blinked and said, 'The very same. You don't mean that you knew him?'

'We used to ride together down El Paso way.'

Szabo who had sized Tango up by now said, 'You must have been a pair to draw to.'

Tango was silent for a while, staring into his coffee cup, then he said to me, 'It must have been someone very good with a gun to take down Curly.'

'They ambushed him,' I told him. 'Took him down like a dog.'

Szabo sensed that there was danger in the air. He tried to smile, and then went on to explain how matters stood out on Diamond now. 'The first thing Grant did when he got back, Montana, he and Bettina kicked all of them off the ranch – Tag, little Amy and Laurel.'

'Where are they!' I couldn't keep the rage out of my voice or my eyes.

'They're all right, Montana, they're here in town. Bettina and Grant Bellows, Cole too are acting like the royalty of the North Country, buying up everything in sight, sneering at the rest of us.'

Drew Tango had been long silent, but now he again lifted his cold blue eyes. He had heard enough.

'Gentlemen,' he said, 'let's have at it. Let's run these vermin to ground.'

First things first: Szabo was without a mount. In a shamefaced way he admitted, 'I'm down to a single silver dollar again, Montana.'

'I've got forty-five dollars left,' I told him. 'Think you can find a horse worth forking for that?'

'Montana, I don't. . . .'

'It was money I was saving back to find a horse for myself, but now that I've got Santana again. . . .'

'I'd appreciate it. What's a cowhand without a pony? I can find something worth riding for that much.'

I thought that he eyed the sleek young Santana and Drew Tango's prancing palomino a little enviously, but there was nothing that could be done about that. Szabo needed only a serviceable horse to keep him with us as we rode up to Diamond. Before he left for the stable to find a horse, I privately asked him my question and he answered. I nodded my response and went back to swing aboard Santana.

'Where are we going?' Tango asked with curiosity as

I started Santana up the street.

'There are some kids I need to see. And. . . .'

'And Laurel?' Tango asked with a laugh.

'I talk too much, don't I,' I said through tight lips.

'Montana,' Tango said, 'don't be ashamed of your finer feelings.'

And he was right. Having made arrangements to meet up again with Szabo, we guided our horses into a narrow side street named Poplar Way and found the house where Laurel and the kids were staying. Tango was right – it felt better to see new life, the promise of a better life ahead to dwell on the man who now lay dead back in the railroad corral. Tracking down Jason Grier had once been the most important objective of my life. Now, he did not matter at all.

The house was small and painted white. Snow drifted past the trellis where a struggling thorny bougainvillea grew. Laurel stood in the doorway watching as we swung down from our horses.

'I'll wait out here,' Drew Tango said, tilting his hat back. He was still grinning. I walked toward Laurel, and without meaning to, I folded her up in my arms in a sort of clumsy embrace. She did not pull away, but only said:

'My, you do take your time about things, don't you?'

'I got side-tracked back in Missouri,' I apologized, but she shook her head.

'That isn't what I meant, Brian.'

What she meant exactly got interrupted by two cheering children's voices. As Laurel showed me into the house, Tango waiting near the white picket fence with his horse, Tag and Amy rushed out of an inner room to meet me.

'Hello, McCulloch,' Tag said in that almost-grown up voice he sometimes assumed.

'Hello, pal, I guess you never thought I'd make it back.'

'McCulloch,' he said seriously, 'I always knew that if anyone could make it back, it would be you.'

'Amy!' Laurel said, hoisting the little girl in the pink dress high. 'You remember Mr McCulloch, don't you?'

'Yes,' Amy answered solemnly. 'He's the man who feeds me only beans.'

The three of us laughed, but Amy did not. It was a small event that had made a deep impression on her young mind. It didn't bother me a bit; I promised her cake and ice cream in the future and she went away smiling. At the kitchen table I told Tag and Laurel some of what had happened recently and some of my plans for the future – if I were to have a future after what I meant to try.

'You're going after him, then?' Laurel asked. 'Grant Bellows and his whole bunch of riders?'

'I have to, don't I?' I responded, glancing at Tag who had his small hands clenched into tight, angry fists.

'I suppose so,' Laurel said wearily. When I looked into her deeply luminous dark brown eyes, she added, 'it's been so wearying, Brian, and there has already been so much pain. I'm not sure if I could handle it if you got yourself killed on top of everything.'

'I'm not going to get killed,' I said with much more confidence than I actually felt. 'I've got Szabo riding with me, and Tango – you don't know him, but he is a good man, and a panther in a fight.' I asked Laurel:

'What did happen with the children's estate and the deed Grant Bellows claims to have. Szabo told me that he is sure it must have been forged.'

'Of course it was forged!' Laurel erupted. She calmed herself, her lip trembling. She looked at Tag. 'There wasn't even a date affixed, Brian. What sort of lawyer would draw up such a document?'

'I suppose that there's many,' I answered sadly. 'But what about the judge who appointed you conservator? Can't he do anything about this?'

'Oh, I don't know!' Laurel said. 'I've tried and tried. I can't tell you how many times I've been down to the courthouse. But the judge was away and I need a lawyer myself to press the case, and you know I have no money to pursue matters.'

'It must have been tough,' I said. 'I'm sorry I wasn't here to share your burden.'

Her hand touched mine across the table, and her dark eyes brightened. 'It wasn't your fault, Brian. We all did what we could.'

'It'll all change now,' Tag said enthusiastically. He pushed away from the table. 'I'm ready to ride, Brian. Old Bitterroot is rested and fit to run.'

'Tag,' I had to tell him, 'you can't go. There will be gunplay. I can't let you get involved in this.'

He started to argue, got no reinforcement from Laurel and sagged into his chair again, disappointment obvious.

'There's too much time ahead of you, Tag,' I said.

'You'll have to run the Diamond from now on, and that's a big enough task.'

'I guess . . .' he shrugged, biting at his lip. 'But I'd sure like to take care of those people who stole Diamond from us.'

'Tag,' I answered, 'revenge would not give you the satisfaction that you think it would. Just grow up strong and proud and take care of your little sister . . . and Laurel.'

Laurel said nothing to me before I left, nor did we so much as touch hands, but I imagined I could feel the warmth of her gaze on my back as I walked out to where Tango still waited. Szabo had caught up with us and now sat in the saddle of a runty, wall-eyed roan horse. I must have shaken my head slightly, for Szabo grumbled:

'What did you expect for forty bucks?'

I didn't answer. I swung into leather aboard Santana and we talked as we rode northward. The snowstorm was fitful, seeming undecided in its purpose. Snowflakes fell in widely separated patches and then the sky would clear to show bright blue in between the pale clouds. The wind – well it blew, and hard.

We spoke as we rode.

'Which of them is the most dangerous?' Drew Tango asked me.

'I suppose Cole has the quickest gun, but there's a man called Gordon Blaine riding with them, and he's pure snake. He's the one who gunned down Curly Sledge, and he didn't balk at the idea of trying to do the same to the children.'

Tango nodded his understanding and disgust. His

143

face brightened and his habitual grin returned.

'Well, men, let's have at it then!' he responded.

And so we pointed our horses' noses toward Diamond, riding almost in silence except for Szabo who twice voiced his disappointment in not having been able to find his Little Nell in Laramie. We knew he was only talking to keep his mind off of the grim reality of what lay ahead.

'Oh well,' I heard him mutter, 'I wouldn't have had the money to treat her anyway.'

Noon found us crossing onto Diamond land. The snow had abated, but the wind had not. It was cutting-cold across the open grassland. Our own bodies shivered, but our minds were set as coldly on our task.

'I guess,' Tango said, opening his coat for easier access to his revolver, 'we're on the killing grounds now.'

I supposed we were. As we crossed grassland encircled by low pine-studded hills I thought of how Peter and Rose Bellows must have worked and planned to build all of this and leave a proud legacy to their children, how that dream had been taken way – by their deaths and by the treachery of Peter's own brother.

We didn't even see the rifleman who opened up on us from the shelter of the pine forest, but the first nasty slap of a bullet hitting flesh sounded distinctly and we went to the sides of our ponies and heeled them toward the shelter of the pines.

Yes, it seemed we had entered the killing ground.

THIRTEEN

The first bullet had tagged Szabo's new roan horse on the flank. The animal, surprised and in pain, limped on three legs into the pine woods. Tango and I slowed our horses slightly so as not to leave Szabo behind. The big man was cursing himself, the rifleman and the universe at large.

I heard him say, 'Poor little pony, I have him for half a day and my bad luck hits him too.'

Reaching the forest we swung down urgently, both Tango and I reaching for our long guns.

There were no more following shots. Tango glanced at me and said, 'What do you want to do, Montana?'

'You're the fighting man,' I answered.

'Yes, but this is not my sort of fight,' he answered 'I'm used to being able to look in my man's eyes. Whoever's shooting – I can't even see him.'

I was no army general myself, but I knew we had to make a decision. The rifleman might have been alone, but as his shots echoed across the valley below us it could bring other riders. We could not remain pinned down where we were. It was Szabo who echoed my

145

thoughts, saying: 'Let's make a run for the ranch. At least there we'll know who we're fighting.'

Tango agreed a little reluctantly. 'I'd rather see my man face to face. Being sniped at . . . well, let's try for the ranch. Is there a trail through the woods?'

'I know the way,' Szabo said. 'If my horse can make it, I'll get us there.' He looked up into the cold, gathering skies. 'You two had better stay close behind me. It's looking like a real squall and you don't want to get lost out here if it blows in hard.'

Szabo had hardly said that when the snow began to intensify, sheeting down through the ranks of the tall pines. I blinked the cold away and followed on, Szabo's wounded little pony only a dark shadow ahead of me. We did not speak for obvious reasons, but we tried to stay close together as the long plains were enveloped by blizzard-strength winds and snow so thick we could barely penetrate it with our vision. I tugged my hat lower yet and stuck as close to the limping roan horse Szabo rode as possible.

The blinding weather would not let up. Trees creaked around us, dropped loose branches and pine cones. A big pine limb exploded in the wind not far from us and we all cringed, taking it at first for another shot taken by the ambusher. After half a mile the wind weakened, but the snow did not abate. We were three dark shadows moving through a white world. No animals moved in the forest, no bird dared to take to wing. The wind, holding back somewhat, still whined eerily through the long stand of pines. I was happy that we had found Szabo to take the lead on the trail. His many years on Diamond had guided him to little-used trails Tango and I could never have found or followed on our own.

As we crested a low knoll the clouds parted as if someone had drawn the drapes and we were looking directly down at the Diamond ranch house. Sitting in the snow-covered valley, barren black oak trees before it, it held no sign of human life that I could see.

'What do you think, Tango?'

'They could have all ridden out to help the ambusher, or they could all be hidden somewhere – in the house, the barn or the bunkhouse.'

I asked Szabo, 'What do you want to do?'

'We're going to have to go down there,' Szabo replied, 'else what was the point in riding out here? I say we split up for now.' He pointed a stubby finger at the ranch, 'Probably the bunkhouse is where we should meet, wouldn't you say?'

'Seems like a plan,' I muttered. How good a plan it was, I did not know. I knew that Szabo was thinking that the familiar bunkhouse was a place where we could possibly find a friendly face if any remained on the ranch. We rode down off the crest of the hill and onto the snow-carpeted valley floor, each of us taking a different route to our destination.

The bunkhouse did not seem promising to me; no smoke rose from its black iron stovepipe, but if we made it to shelter, we at least had a chance of pausing to organize a plan to defeat Grant Bellows, Cole and Gordie Blaine along with whoever else might be riding with them. I was wondering – so was Szabo, I guessed –

if Sylvester and Turkey, any of the old hands were still around to be counted on. They would not have started a fight on their own, it would have been suicidal for them to do so, but if they were willing we might be able to talk them into joining us now.

No shots rang out as we approached the ranch. Santana's hoofs passed over the snowy ground in eerie silence. Once, glancing toward the house as I circled south, away from Tango and Szabo, I thought I saw, briefly, the dark figure of a woman moving behind one of the curtained windows. Well, Bettina would be there, wouldn't she?

Still, I couldn't be sure from that brief glimpse if it was her or the shadows of the day, the swirl of the steadily falling snow, playing tricks with my vision. I had lost sight of Szabo and Tango as they passed the other side of the house, and I saw no one lurking behind the barn doors or in the hayloft. Nothing, not a ghost of a shadow moved through the storm. Santana, perhaps smelling fresh hay, started to turn toward the barn, but we veered away. I stroked his sleek, cold neck mentally promising him that there would be better days ahead.

If we could survive this one.

Approaching the bunkhouse I saw a moving shadow, twitched and started to raise my Winchester, but it was only Szabo trailing in from the north side of the house, Drew Tango flanked out to his side.

Well then, here we were. But what was waiting inside the bunkhouse? Men with guns, old friends, cold emptiness with the riders behind us ready to circle the building and pepper away at us with their rifles until we had no chance but to surrender or be gunned down?

I drew up at the hitch rail, looping Santana's reins loosely around it. I kept my rifle in my hand as I watched Tango and Szabo from the corner of my eye, dismount and tie their own horses. Szabo briefly examined his pony's flank and shook his head. There was nothing that could be done about the wound just now.

The three of us glanced at one another. No one was eager to open the bunkhouse door to discover what lay behind it, but as Szabo had said, we had to do it or else there was no point in coming out here. I stepped up onto the frosted porch, took in a slow breath, and whirled with my rifle still in my hands, kicking the door open, Szabo and Drew Tango nearly at my heels.

'Hello, boys,' Turkey said as we entered. 'You've been away for some time.'

The old man sat huddled on his bunk, wrapped in his blankets. No fire burned in the iron stove although there was a small stack of split wood beside it. Turkey looked much older and appeared sick.

'Why don't you have a fire?' I asked with concern. He looked up and shook his head.

'Cole's orders. No fire.'

Szabo scowled, walked to the stove, squatted on his heels and began to build a fire. 'What's he want you to do, save the wood until spring?'

'I don't ask Art Cole what he's thinking,' Turkey said. 'I just do what he tells me.' He smiled, weakly, 'It keeps me alive, doing as I'm told.'

'Are things that bad up here?' I asked.

149

'Real bad, Montana. Real bad.' He scooted a little nearer to the fire which was beginning to burn brightly. 'Laurel and the kids. . . .'

'We saw them in Laramie,' I told the old man. 'They're all right, but they don't have the money to survive on for long.'

'No, I reckon not,' Turkey said. 'They wouldn't have given her even a little of the money from the cattle sale, would they?'

'Who did get it?' Szabo asked, unbuttoning his heavy sheepskin coat now that the fire had been started. Turkey shrugged.

'Don't ask me. I believe Bellow, Cole and Gordie Blaine made a three-way split, but who got the fattest share, I don't know.'

'Why Blaine?' I asked. I understood Cole – he had been the Diamond's foreman, and Bellows would not wish to antagonize the dark-eyed gunman anyway.

'Because you were right,' Turkey told me, raising his eyes to meet mine. 'Blaine made sure that there was an accident so that Peter and Rose Bellows would both be killed. He was tracking the kids down to do the same. With what he knows, Grant Bellows would have to pay him off or risk having Blaine tell the law what happened.'

I wanted to discuss the matter further, but Drew Tango was interested in more concrete problems. 'Where is everybody? Have they got gunmen hidden out around the ranch?'

'There's nobody left,' Turkey said, rubbing his gnarled hands together at the stove. 'The Collier boys, they pulled out after they got to Laramie. I don't know if Grant Bellows even paid them their wages. Sylvester . . . well soon after you two left,' he nodded at Szabo and at me, 'it seems that something happened to the kid. . . .' He shook his head sadly. 'I don't know for sure what happened; I wasn't there, but he's probably dead. I heard Cole and Grant talking about him once while I was over behind the house scrounging wood. They seem to think that because I'm old I also must be deaf. Sylvester, he was a good kid. It's just a pity the way it all worked out.' He went on more quietly:

'Just a damn shame. Diamond used to be a fine spread, one that men were proud to be riding for.'

'It will be again!' I found myself saying fiercely without any real justification. Turkey glanced up once more, surprised at the strength of my outburst.

'Let's hope so, Montana. Let's hope that it can happen . . . for the sake of the kids.'

Perhaps because he was a little distanced from the troubles of Diamond, Tango again took things to a more practical level. 'What's to eat, Turkey? You look like you could use some nourishment yourself. And I think one of us had better go over to the window to keep an eye on things. Have you got a weapon, old-timer?'

'My scattergun behind my bunk,' Turkey answered.

'You'd better keep it near at hand now – if you're in this fight with us.'

Minutes later Turkey had his shotgun across his narrow lap, a small pile of spare shells mounded beside him on his bunk's blanket. Drew Tango stood at the window, keeping watch as the snow continued to swirl past the window. In his hand was an open can of cold beans which he spooned into his mouth quickly as if he might be taking his last meal.

Maybe he was, I considered.

'They'll know we're here,' Szabo said heavily. 'For one thing,' he nodded toward the stove, 'that smoke will tip them off. Then if the new snow isn't covering our tracks. . . .'

'I'd better get the horses around to the back,' Drew Tango said. 'That might give us a little extra time to get organized.' He tossed the empty can into a box provided for them and started out into the storm again.

'You say there's only the three of them now?' Szabo wanted to know.

'That's right – just Grant Bellows, Cole and Gordie Blaine,' Turkey answered. They didn't figure that they'd need anybody else around with the herd gone and with you and Montana taken care of.'

'Are you sure they didn't hire anyone else, Turkey?' I asked with concern. Turkey seemed to be well-informed, but locked up in the bunkhouse as he had been lately he couldn't possibly know everything that had been going on.

'Not that I know of,' he said, looking at me with badly frightened eyes. 'They could have, though. If they found out that you were back in Laramie. . . .'

Drew Tango came back in the front door, letting a gust of cold wind arrive with him. He stamped the snow from his boots and told us, 'I didn't see them anywhere, but through that snow you can't see much.'

'All right, then,' Szabo said with a frown, 'let's set up our position and wait for them to come in. They'll be mad as hell and ready to fight for sure. They won't want to risk losing what they've spent all this time and energy stealing.'

None of us was prepared for what happened next. The door to the bunkhouse was kicked open and we saw Art Cole standing there, his hat tied down, his sheepskin coat buttoned to the throat.

'Damnit Turkey, didn't I tell you. . . .'

Then Cole's eyes flickered as he realized the situation he had walked into. Turkey was there and the three of us, all armed. Art Cole moved first, but he was no more prepared to shoot than anyone else. He pawed at his Colt, trying to find it beneath his coat flaps. Tango gave him half a chance and then drilled the ranch foreman with two rapidly fired and well-aimed shots. Cole staggered backward, his arms moving like windmills and he fell on his back onto the snow outside.

In his excitement, Turkey had dropped his shotgun behind his bunk. Szabo was still unbuttoning his coat and I had not even made a move as Drew Tango took care of business for all of us.

'Pretty quick with that, aren't you?' Szabo asked, perhaps wondering for the first time who and what Drew Tango was. Tango didn't bother to answer, but did smile faintly as he thumbed two fresh cartridges into the cylinder of his revolver.

'I think . . . Turkey said, rising to his feet, his retrieved scattergun in his hand.

It didn't matter what Turkey thought. The

bunkhouse was rapidly filling with smoke: someone had clogged up the stovepipe. They had either heard Tango's shots or discovered our horses tied out back. But they had decided to smoke us out. And when we bolted from the smoke-filled building, there would be guns trained on us from out of the concealing wash of snow.

The smoke was already thick, rolling up toward the bare ceiling and hanging there in dark clouds. I could feel its heat in my lungs. Tango had taken off his bandana and now held it across his face and nose. He removed it long enough to say:

'The time to get out is now, boys. The only question is who's going to try it first.'

I looked toward the doorway, but Szabo had already started that way. I moved up close on his heels. The first man out would take the brunt of the attack; the second man would have a chance of spotting their muzzle flashes and firing back through the gloom and swirl of the storm.

'One at a time!' Turkey howled, 'we'll be like a row of ducks in a shooting gallery.'

He was right, but there was nothing that we could do about it. The woodsmoke in the interior of the bunkhouse was lowering, suffocating us. I heard Szabo give a yell in some language that was not English, saw him leap through the door, his handgun blazing away at targets he could never have seen.

I followed him, rushing from the black clouds of smoke into the smothering white of the blizzard.

FOURTEEN

I saw Szabo lurch to one side of me as he leaped from the porch into the snow. I saw him spin, stagger and I knew he was hit. I made out a single muzzle blast, a stabbing tongue of flame from behind the oaks and I winged a shot that way, but I did not stop running. Inconsequentially my mind registered that the weapon had the distinctive crack of a Winchester and I knew that they had positioned themselves for rifle fire. It was hardly surprising – Gordon Blaine was at his best as an ambusher firing from cover.

I didn't know if Szabo was alive; didn't know if Drew Tango had even made it out the front door. I plunged on across the snowfield, staggering, slipping, stumbling. I had few options, and I had decided to run toward the ranch house. I would have cover there. The house was still dark; no lantern burned in the windows. I did not know the house well, but I had been in it and I thought I was familiar enough with it to use its walls' protection once I got inside.

I shouldered through the kitchen door, hit the floor heavily and looked around, gasping, my Colt feeling cold and clumsy in my hand, my thumb hooked over the hammer. No one was there. No sound above the constant rush of the storm could be heard. I scraped myself to my feet and crossed the kitchen where once I had sat watching Laurel at her tasks, thinking that it was the finest, most comfortable room that could be imagined on this cold planet.

I stepped into the hallway beyond, holding my Colt up beside my ear, muzzle toward the ceiling. I still heard nothing, saw no shadow of movement as I crept forward down the dark corridor. I thought I heard more shots being fired beyond the walls of the house, but all sounds and movements were muffled and hidden by the swirl of the blizzard. In nearly complete darkness I eased toward the front room, wanting to get to the windows to watch the yard and keep Grant Bellows and Gordie Blaine from returning to the house, and I was beginning to believe that they would be forced to try for it.

I had no idea of how much ammunition they were carrying, if they had spent it all, but even if that was not a consideration, no one was going to last long in the heart of this blizzard without shelter. The storm had not abated, but seemed to have increased in its fury, clawing and raging against the walls of the house. The very floor of the place trembled under my feet.

It was cold in the room, not much warmer than it had been outside, but at least the savage wind was cut by the structure's walls.

'Hold it,' the voice behind me cautioned, and in the darkness I could make out the silhouette of a woman and the shotgun that Bettina Bellows held. 'I knew from the first time I saw you that you would be trouble, McCulloch.'

The door to the front burst open and I saw the wild-eyed Grant Bellows burst through. The rifle in his hands went to his shoulder and I dove for the floor. The rifle touched off and I heard a piercing scream. Bellows had missed me, but Bettina had been standing directly behind me and his bullet had tagged her. The report of the rifle shot was still echoing in my ears when I heard two more shots fired close at hand. I rolled over and scrambled to my feet to see Tango standing there. In the doorway Grant Bellows lay dead and cold, the blowing snow drifting over his still form.

Tango walked forward, frowning. 'What happened to her?' he asked me, but I was looking past Tango at the shadow of a man in the hallway behind him. I crouched and brought my revolver up, triggering two rounds through its barrel. Tango swung around in time to watch as Gordon Blaine slowly slid to the floor, his fingers clawing at the wall.

Tango walked towards him cautiously, bent over and then shook his head. 'He's dead. He must have followed me in the back door.' Then he smiled, just slightly. 'Your shooting is improving some, Montana.'

I found a lantern and lit it, dragged Grant Bellows' body aside and closed the door to the gusting wind. Drew Tango found some wood and started a fire in the big stone fireplace of the ranch house. Belatedly, Turkey wandered in from the back door, looking like some lonely spirit cast out by the storm. He had his blanket clutched tightly around his shoulders. He walked to the fire, placed his shotgun aside, glanced at the motionless form of Bettina Bellows, her blond hair spread out across the wooden floor, and wagged his head, seating himself on one of the black leather chairs.

'Where's Szabo?' I asked, and Turkey had to tell me:

'He's dead. He never made it across the yard.'

The three of us sat in silence for a long while, firelight shadowing our faces, the dead lying too near to us for our comfort. Still no one wished to rise from the warmth of the fire and so we remained where we were, not speaking, only staring at the curling flames. After a while I noticed that Drew Tango had fallen asleep, his arms folded across his chest, hat pulled down over his eyes. Turkey appeared to have dozed off as well. I could not sleep, however; I rose and fed the fire from time to time and sat in my chair, watching the twisting red and gold flames rise to expend their heat futilely against the cold fury of the long storm.

In the morning we removed the dead. Outside the sky was blue between the huge parting white clouds. We found Szabo and moved him as well. The day appeared bright, but its mood was somber.

We talked little. Finally at noon when it was obvious we would have to eat soon or perish, Turkey found supplies in the kitchen and made us ham sandwiches which we took out onto the front porch of the ranch house.

'What do you plan to do now, Tango?' I asked the blond railroad detective.

'Me? I'll be going home. That is, to the railroad. It's funny how much being out in the cold and wind up here has made me appreciate the warmth of those Pullman cars. I happen to like riding the rails, Montana. Like any other job I get tired of it sometimes, but it's my life. The railroad's my home.'

'What about you Turkey?'

'Me?' the old man looked surprised. He swallowed a bite of his sandwich and answered. 'Well, I *am* home, Montana. I figure on dying right here on Diamond, and that's just fine with me. I have no wish to go adventuring at my age. What's your plan?'

'I don't know,' I answered honestly. 'I suppose I'll be going home, too. The Montana trail will still be plenty rugged this time of year, but I think I can make it back to where I belong. The only place I ever called home.' I was thinking of the long lonely trek, of another cold winter in the cabin which would be even more lonely with Sad Sam gone. Tango said:

'You'd better hold back for a little while.' He lifted his chin toward the Laramie road and as I watched, here came Laurel driving a buckboard, and beside her rode Tag and little Amy. I got to my feet. 'You might find out that you're already home too.'

I was still standing there when a few minutes later Laurel drove the buckboard into the snowy yard of Diamond ranch. The wind was shifting her dark hair and shuffling the folds of her blue skirt. She hesitated before she tied the reins off around the brake handle. Hesitated again as she stepped down from the buckboard and saw me waiting across the yard.

But the children did not. Tag gave out yell of delight and ran toward me across the yard, little Amy trying to keep up with him. Tag reached me, started to shake hands and then threw his arms around me. Amy was there as well, clinging to my leg, looking up at me with her intent blue eyes.

'Come on kids, you must be tired and cold,' I said.

I turned toward the house, taking one of Tag's hands, one of Amy's and led them that way. I glanced across my shoulder and saw Laurel, smiling happily, walking after us as I led the kids back up the porch into their old home.

My new home.